THE JOTS
&TITTLES
OF SCRIBES AND STORYTELLERS
II

The Jots & Tittles of Scribes and Storytellers: Volume II

ISBN: 978-0-9980734-2-2

Published in the United States of America

This book is dedicated to all of the emerging authors who have a story to tell... but nowhere to tell it.

Then He said to them, *"Therefore every scribe instructed concerning the kingdom of heaven is like a householder who brings out of his treasure things new and old."*

$\sim$ Jesus; the Ultimate Storyteller
(Matthew 13:52)

TABLE OF CONTENTS

STAYING UNDER THE INFLUENCE
A Story of Escape, Surrender, and Capture

Sandra Astacio

LOVE NEVER FAILS
The Book of Faith

Elaine Roundtree Montford and Elder
D.H.Bonner

THE ADVENTURES OF CHANDLER & THE TRAVELING PRAYER SHAWL
Shelly Shelton

A BASKET OF EMPTY PROMISES
Angel Miller

TWO HEARTS UNITED
Tamala Coleman

ABOUT THE AUTHORS

STAYING UNDER THE INFLUENCE

SANDRA ASTACIO

PROLOGUE

The tall sugar cane rods and heavy underbrush made for not only a soft place to rest, but also shelter from the heavy raindrops as they began to fall. She could hear the distant shout of her name being called and tried desperately to steady her breathing enough to not give away her location. Amid the rainfall, the shouts became more desperate and angrier. Perhaps they were starting to become concerned for her safety on the forefront of what looked like a typical summer thunderstorm. But, nevertheless, she didn't move a muscle. She shrunk herself down among the brush to escape what she thought would take an eagle eye to spot her. What she didn't realize was that the haze that the rain gifted helped her escape the view of her abuser. For now.

The familiar taste of tears began to wash over her face as she now realized the pain in her side was making it even more difficult to steady her breathing. It was sharp. Stabbing. Maybe a rib was broken this time? That shoe was thrown hard and as usual, landed on its intended target. As usual. Yes, as usual.

When the rain subsided, she could hear the engine start on the muscle car and knew that he was ready to continue his search. Of course, the way he vainly thought of his hair, there was no way he was going to venture out and get it wet, so waiting until the rain subsided was expected. Knowing that dusk was approaching, the headlights might reflect off her glasses, so she had to make a quick decision. Did she move or did she risk getting hurt even more by taking her glasses off and not seeing a snake or other small animal approach? She wondered how the natives used to do it. She recalled the last history lesson she learned earlier that week and suddenly a panic swept over her. "What if my teacher misses me next week? What if my teacher actually sees my bruises?" Somehow it had to stop. It had to be okay. It was only Friday and there were only two days left. She wondered if the pain in her side would go away by then so she could play kickball during recess on Monday.

The car approached the wooded area and she took off her glasses, laid flat on the ground and held her breath. She recognized the sound of fishtailing down the dirt road and felt the pellets of hardened mud hit her back. He wasn't slowing down and she, although scared for her life, began to smile. She knew that his not slowing down meant that he would *keep going*! This was her chance!

Once the muffler roar faded in the distance, the coast was clear. With one swift movement, she stood up, placed her glasses back on her rain-soaked face, wiped her muddy hair out of her eyes and began to sprint back towards the house. Her side was on fire and the pain in her lungs was as if she was running in the dead of winter down a long winding trail. But it was summer; hot, muggy, and still sprinkling. Making it to the front porch, she landed on the instep of the front door only to find it locked. BAM! Her frail little body slammed against the door, her wrist contorting as it was met with an unyielding knob. Her face fell hard against the floral wreath that was nailed to the outside of the door and she *just missed* the rusty nail as it hit the brim of her glasses!

Not a second to spare, she headed around the back of the house to find his bedroom window open a bit. Of course, it was to let the pot smoke out, she thought as she shoved her finger aside the screen and popped it out of the frame. Reaching above her head, she pushed up the rusted window, hearing the dirt drag along the inside track. With just enough of it open, she had to take a couple of steps back and make a running leap to hoist herself into the window. Stepping on the ripened mulberries that littered the back yard, she just KNEW he would see her purple shoe prints all over his bedspread and know she shimmied the window open to get in.

Running out of time, she decided not to take off her shoes. Instead, she mustered her strength, ran at the side of the house and in one tall leap, landed headfirst inside the window onto the hard, wooden floor. Amelia then brought her legs in, climbed over the fast food tray on the bed full of pot seeds, and made it to the door. She opened it wide and ran to the front room to check the clock. Her mom was due home any minute. She ran back to her brother's room and closed the window only a few inches. Then, she ran back outside and carefully replaced the screen into her brother's window. She also wiped up her mulberry-stained shoe prints on the floor.

She glanced back onto the bed and saw that not one seed rolled onto the bedspread. She smiled and closed the door to his room. Ripping off her clothes, she ran to the only bathroom to take a shower. She then caught a glimpse of herself in the mirror. It was a face she didn't recognize. The way she hid. The way she ran. The way she leaped into the window like some stunt woman she watched on TV. How she literally cleared her tracks on the floor. The way she was timing her shower, placing her wet clothes and shoes in the washer along with a load of towels to hide more *evidence*. The way she scanned the living room for turned-over tables and lamps, or any shards of glass. The cover-up was successful; at least for now. The bruise was already purple on her side, just like her feet. But there was something different about this face. The scared little girl just crossed over into something else. She just became something different. Little did she know; she just changed the odds forever.

She became a fighter.

FAR FROM ORDINARY

*A*melia was not an ordinary woman. She was born into a life of poverty, addiction, sexual perversion, abuse, and abandonment. From the earliest days that she could remember, there was always a void in her heart that she never could fill. Every part of her wanted to blame it on her dad for leaving so early and being such a narcissist, he never truly came to understand who she was or what her needs were. He never stood up for her or pulled her out of harm's way from her older brother Bruce.

Even after Bruce's overdose, her dad never spoke of the real reason he left, why he rarely returned for visits or exactly how much of Bruce's abuse he knew of. He just acted like it didn't exist and what was done was done. From his perspective, finding *'That Jesus'* allegedly changed him into this great guy who was categorically different in every aspect of the man she knew left that hot summer morning decades before. Although she was briefly introduced to his faith years earlier, she didn't hold to the belief that *her dad's religion* was going to welcome her anyway. At least, not now. Not in the condition she was in.

Visions clouded her mind at all times. Visions of good times and of bad times that seemed so normal for her family. She could remember the heat of the summer and the gardenias outside of her window, filling her room with their heavenly fragrance. She recalled the sting of the sun on her shoulders as she played on the old tire swing in her neighbor's yard. Her goal was to swing high enough to where she could reach the tops of the trees, where the sun's rays were always peeking through. She would sing original songs to an invisible audience. The songs were always songs that spoke of her future freedom from where she was. They were songs that beckoned '*That Jesus*' her mom spoke of who would somehow hear her wishes and deliver her from the life she knew.

Since it rained every afternoon in the summer, she wouldn't get off the swing until it was a heavy sprinkle. Those were the days that the daredevil in her would rear its head. She often kept pushing the envelope as she grew, taking bold risks and not letting anyone else push her around. She created a fighting spirit within her that had no life expectancy.

This same fighting spirit made her eventually outwit her brother, avoiding him for days and then eventually, cutting him out of her life for good. This same fighting spirit allowed her to not listen to her mother's excuses of failing to run interference more often and it also stood in for her father's ambivalence. This free and reckless nature coupled dangerously with that fighting spirit. It did, ironically, help her come finally to moments of great escape from scenarios that would later prove that her judgment was off, as she frequently placed herself in the wrong hands. When the voices inside her heart and her head were shouting at her to leave the bad situations, the dysfunctional jobs or even the very people that brought it all on, the shouts had to be louder than the music or she wouldn't listen!

Like the abuse that she gravitated towards, she also was familiar with betrayal. Losing track of her closest friend in her teens and never having someone in her life that she could truly count on, she relied only on herself. She was fiercely independent, but when it came to sharing her heart (or her body) too soon, she was a master at it. Often, it led her in the direct path of a handsome jerk that would take advantage of her. Wanting so desperately to be accepted, Amelia would befriend others to share her heart with and never recognized that this level of trust or intimacy was not fully reciprocated.

From her earliest memories, there was always an element of rejection, humiliation, or some other form of embarrassment that she could vividly recount. Shaking off the residual feeling of those memories took her almost a lifetime. The following are glimpses into that life until one chance meeting occurred that changed everything.

STEALING THE SHOW

"*I*t's perfect!" she shrieked.

The dress was powder blue with white trim and a pretty bow in the back. The saddle oxfords her mom found a few days before at the local thrift store will complete the outfit. Now, if only her naturally wavy hair will cooperate next week and flip at the ends like Mary Tyler Moore, then she will be a dead ringer for Lucy! Charlie Brown was being played by her heartthrob Jack—but anyone who loved *Peanuts* knows that Charlie Brown was never into Lucy! It was always that *little red-haired girl*. That character wasn't in *this* Christmas school play, but nevertheless, she couldn't steal Jack's heart. She would, however, strive to steal the show!

Weeks of rehearsing her lines and the anticipation was building. When it was time for music class, she darted ahead to get to the front. When it was time to practice the lines and take directions from Ms. Wembley, little Amelia prided herself as a 'star in the making' and always a consummate professional. After all, she had already been told by Ms. Wembley that she was a natural at acting, had great stage presence, and could hold a note when asked to sing! This play was her shot at being recognized as a serious student or more importantly, a serious *human being*. Perhaps they wouldn't make fun of her hair, her skin tone, her buck teeth, or her bottle-lensed glasses once that they saw what a great actress she was becoming.

One could only hope.

The best part of this whole day was that she didn't have to share this experience with her brother. He always had a way of homing in on anyone else's happiness and single-handedly destroying it. It seemed jealousy was the gear he was stuck in all the time! He acted out towards her as she was the 'baby' and took up most of their mom's energy and time. And the preparation it was taking for this Christmas play was no exception. Lucky for Amelia, Bruce was hanging out at the mall with his friends and wouldn't be coming with her and her mom to the play. She had secretly hoped that he could come, just to see how good she was and show him that other people did like her. Contrary to what he always said, she was smart, funny, and did have talent. If only he would care about her as a person and not make everything about him for once. But she knew even at this age what a tall order that. Wise beyond her years, this girl was. Wise.

Almost two hours in curlers and under the heat of a portable hairdryer, Amelia surfaced with a perfect *flip*! Her mom coated her hair with Aqua Net, helped her zip up the pretty, powder blue dress and tied up her oxfords.

Amelia and her mom arrived at the lunchroom, went through a side door to the stage and met Ms. Wembley at the top of the stairs. Her green eyes widened when she saw Amelia and she smiled at her. She greeted Amelia's mom, motioned for her to go sit in the front row in the auditorium and then hurried Amelia over to her other castmates. Jack was the first person to see her. He had a t-shirt on with a chevron stripe across the chest and his hair was slicked back. He laughed loudly at her hair, but not in a harmful way. He said that without the glasses and how she was dressed, she was the perfect Lucy.

Unfortunately, the other children did not have such a discerning eye for character acting. They let out a raucous laughter and even pointed at her freshly polished oxfords. Amelia wasn't wearing her glasses, so she could only imagine what their faces looked like and quickly looked away. Hot tears filled her eyes, but as she turned away, her eyes locked with Ms. Wembley's. What was just an illuminated smile morphed into a terse frown. She motioned again with her hands towards the other children and the laughter stopped. Amelia waited for her vocal queue as the music was starting and the first scene was hers. Wiping the tears from her eyes, donning a play-perfect smile, and holding her can of air freshener (the magical mystical Christmas spray), she stood ready. "Curtain opens in 5, 4, 3, 2 and, go Lucy!" whispered Ms. Wembley. Glancing back towards her, Amelia's heart skipped a beat as the bright green eyes and glowing smile returned to her teacher's face. Confidently, Amelia strutted out onto the stage...

Each punch line was delivered with a facial expression, a hand on a hip and a palm-up push of her *flip*. The audience roared with laughter, clapped and at the end of the show, stood to their feet! Her mom's silhouette was barely recognizable under the glare of the stage lights, so taking a chance it was her, Amelia blew a kiss towards her. A unified "aww" could be heard, so apparently, Amelia was right! Regardless, she could only do what any 9-year-old would do at this moment — she began to cry. She couldn't stop the tears. She didn't even realize she had that option. She just stood there and wept. The silhouette came closer and reaching over the edge of the stage, Amelia's mom handed her the glasses she couldn't wear for the last hour. That's when she saw their faces. All of them smiling and clapping.

It was a new feeling Amelia had never experienced before. It was a warm feeling and as it overcame her, her tears stopped, and she began to smile. That was the first touch of something that, although unfamiliar to her that day, would later become the very hinge point of her testimony. Feelings like that moment would manifest over the years to come. Unbeknownst to her, none of them would be as genuine and pure as *this* moment.

See, that day, she experienced affirmation in the sincerest form. And it changed her deeply. She began looking for it again but didn't find it until that one fateful day she surrendered her search. Then, she realized that much of what she was being fed was a far cry from what she deserved. Instead, intentions were sinister, calculated, manipulative, masochistic, and fake. And the saddest part was that she never could tell the difference.

IT WAS ONLY A MEMORY

The moonlight was shining the brightest the night Amelia decided to take a huge risk. From the backyard under the large mulberry tree, the shadows of the leaves made a pattern on the cool grass under her bare feet. Her friend's giggles were steadily getting louder as *both* their hearts raced! At the edge of the yard was the VW bug that the guys were in, waiting for them. No one ever said that 8th grade would be this exciting!

"Come on," he whispered while waving a bottle of whiskey above his head. Denise, Amelia's friend, suddenly sprouted wings it seemed and darted towards the car ahead of her. She was always the more impetuous one, Amelia thought. She introduced her to those little pink pills during science class, showed her how easy it was to steal the blue, excused permission slips from the front office to effortlessly skip class. Now, she knew in her gut that *this risk* was the biggest one of all — sneaking out on New Year's Eve with a bunch of boys, booze, and an intent to throw reckless abandon to the winds!

The warmth of the fire was soothing and although she was still barefoot, the music kept her dancing the cool nip of the night away! In the distance, she heard fireworks and somehow that provoked a loud "yeehaw!" each time. There it was, the payoff she was looking for. The ability to shout at the top of her lungs and no one would hear her. Except this time, it was shouts of release, joy, laughter, and a celebratory cry of owning what seemed like *forever*. For once, her shouts and cries were not from a place of pain or horror, but from a place she didn't know existed within her.

Hours had passed and over the rooftops of the new home construction behind her neighborhood, the sky began to turn a familiar shade of crimson. Around her lay her buddies, curled up near the fire, asleep on the dirt. Everyone except Denise. She knew the VW was still parked up the path, so she ran towards the open road. Denise was lying on the side of the road. It was a wonder, not *a miracle*, that no one had passed by the construction site and witnessed this young girl laying on the ground!

"Get up!" Amelia shouted. "We have to head back... NOW! Denise, Get up!"

But she didn't move. Amelia placed her hands over her face and felt air. Relieved, but not willing to delay any further, she shook Denise until she woke up. Frantic because of the increasing sunlight, Amelia grabbed her friend's arm and they both began to run. Although they stopped every few minutes to throw up, they kept running until they reached the edge of the yard.

There he stood. On the front porch with a scowl on his face. He shouted for them *both* to meet him around back to get cleaned up before coming back into the house. Scared, but grateful for the help, they ran around back. Bruce met them at the stairs. With a fierce growl, he grabbed Amelia and shoved her inside the kitchen. She heard a loud thud then felt the piercing pain behind her left eye.

Suddenly, there was that moonlight again. The light was almost blinding! All Amelia could hear was a faint biding, "get up! Come on, now, get up!" Except it wasn't *her* voice and it wasn't Bruce's. She then realized that Denise was not there. Denise had not been seen in years. The memory was so vivid that she didn't realize she was asleep!

Shaking her head, she saw the light again, beaming into her eyes. The officer was shining a flashlight into her backseat where she was laying. She rolled down the window and there stood a familiar face. It was Keith. Her brother grew up with him and he knew her. He received the call from one of the neighbors that a car was parked in the ditch. He recognized the street name, so he came quickly. She was parked in front of her mother's house, on the other side of the mulberry tree and back bumper down towards the ditch. Her keys were still in the ignition and the windows were fogged. No shoes on her feet and the smell of stale alcohol and cigarettes filled the air.

She felt the sting of the cold air rushing through the open window. Luckily, Keith was used to seeing her like this. He had seen the nights Bruce had close calls like this one and it was no surprise Amelia was repeating the same pattern. Unlocking the driver door, Keith jumped in, started it up and drove it around the corner to the front yard. He reached over and rolled down the passenger window, shaking his head in disappointment. Turning towards her still in the backseat he said, "you're better than this, girl. I know your mama and if she saw you like this, it would kill her. Get it together. Vacuum this thing out, spray some disinfectant, do anything you can to get this right. Next time, you may not be so lucky." Leaving the driver door open, Keith walked to his squad car and left.

He was right. Amelia knew there was an opportunity awaiting her to escape it all. She knew that another 'wrong' would not make a 'right,' but she knew that if she had to steal, lie, and cheat her way to *this point*, she could do it *one last time* to get out. And get out *for good*.

"THAT JESUS"

$\mathcal{A}$melia's dad probably sang the loudest in the church that morning. She could see how other teenage girls would point and giggle at her and the 'old Amelia' would have taken care of them by now, but something inside her was keeping her planted firmly in the pew next to her dad. It was her senior year in school and although she didn't know a soul at this new school, she was determined to reinvent herself for the better! Being seventeen was hard enough without having to explain why she uprooted herself from her home during the most memorable year in her education — her senior year! She wanted everyone in her school to know about how bad things got, but she didn't want pity.

Still not truly understanding how her father just took her in like that, she closed her eyes and remembered that no matter what, he promised her that she would not have to return home. She leaned a little closer to him and he gently placed his head on hers. Goosebumps ran down her arm as the choir started a new song and she began to weep. Who was this Jesus they sang about? Did sitting next to her dad and feeling the safety of his presence resemble the love this Jesus had for God's people? Amelia wondered if this Jesus would be so loving if he knew how she had to steal a great deal of drugs in order to pay for a one-way flight to safety. She wondered if this Jesus knew how scared her mom must have been to learn that her daughter left the state to escape the abuse. A pang of guilt ran through her at that very moment. Suddenly, the goosebumps were gone. And just like that, she doubted He forgave her. Hanging her head, she wept while the choir sang.

The ride home was a good forty-five minutes and unlike the rides before, this one seemed different. The curving mountain roads were the same. The weeping willows were still bright green and the fences along the farms they passed were still a shade of weathered white. Gospel music filled the air in the car and her dad softly hummed along. She couldn't possibly confess to her dad that she was doubting Jesus really loved her, not after all that she had done. She wouldn't tell him how she got the money for the plane ticket and he stopped asking. Deep down she wanted to tell him everything. She wanted to tell him about the nights left alone, the beatings, the drunken drives across the state in the middle of the night and about how she couldn't possibly hold a 3.0 GPA on her own. Given the change in states and requirements, this final senior year would be a breeze.

Little did she know that history sometimes had a way of repeating itself.

Five months went by and although she attended church intermittently, becoming baptized in blue jeans because of some religious mandate she didn't understand, Amelia soon found her way back to the identical crowd she was most familiar with. Sure, their faces were different, but the attitudes were the same. The crime was the same. The drugs and the whiskey were the same, too. She tried to get used to being sober during the regular school day but that wasn't working. She saw that a life of purity wasn't practiced by even her dad, so why was it such a big deal that she skip church again? She often wondered if 'That Jesus' knew she had given up on Him. She often wondered if He even cared.

Within a week after graduation, she was on her way back home. Forfeiting a scholarship to a top university, she opted for a shot at a community college until she figured out if she had what it took to stay in school anyway. Yes, that promise Amelia's dad made to her was broken, but she could hardly blame him. After all, it was only a matter of time that he realized much of his own private stash was missing and the secret would be out. Waiting as the other shoe dropped, she tried to keep the schedule of attending class, working a part-time job, and having any kind of social life. Something had to give because there was no end in sight of the monotony of it all. Another empty promise of hope, perhaps. It reminded her a little of *'That Jesus'* she met years before. How being on that path that others wanted her to stay on would have made her an obedient, but mindless robot. Always doing what others expected and for what? A choir spot? *No thanks*, she thought, *not this girl.* Besides, what if others came asking about her past? How much of that would she have to lie about? Amelia wasn't afraid of the people of the church knowing more about her, she was afraid of *'That Jesus'* rejecting her. So, she rejected Him *first*.

About five years had passed and at barely 23 years old, Amelia would find herself back in a season of change. This time, though, it was with two years of college, four part-time jobs, two car repossessions, and one near-husband experience under her belt. Overall, this season wasn't much different in that she was still running. She was still searching for that feeling she felt that night near the fire, the feeling of owning *'forever'* in bare feet!

Fearing the finality of adulthood, she denied it as much as she could. She went to the beach with her girlfriends, danced all hours of the night on weekends, slept with anyone she wanted to (married or not) and went anywhere she wanted to go. The rush of escape was addicting. She didn't have to talk about Bruce, her former life, or the legacy of nightmares he left behind. She had disregarded the constant attempts he made before his death to connect and she didn't have one ounce of regret. Denying him access into her world all those years gave her a bit of that *'barefoot'* feeling anyhow. She still had to stomach the grief her mom had from time to time, mostly when she would visit on holidays. But she would quickly make a joke to lighten the mood, pour a glass of wine or head to the backyard for a quick toke to avoid the emotion. She would stand on the back porch near his old room. The room was now filled with porcelain dolls and as many flea market-finds as her mom could fit. To her, it was still *his* room.

Gazing at that window, she thought the distance from the ground outside seemed *much greater* back then. She would silently feel grateful that he never knew everything about that day she jumped through his window or about the night she contemplated ending her pain permanently by his bedside. The gun was off the holster and loaded. All she needed were the guts to carry it out.

Amelia had grown accustomed to the flashbacks and the visions. Escape was the only coping mechanism she mastered. The anger of the injustice would begin to seep into her bones and would find its way out of her one way or another! If only they knew of the misery she not only endured, but also of the misery she witnessed successfully nest itself in her mom's life. A misery so invasive, it would likely take her life one day. And with that thought, Amelia was certain she would be left with yet another lineage of memories and unrequited understanding. An unyielding emptiness that even *'That Jesus'* couldn't fill. That's *if* she would let Him.

A DOUBLE BETRAYAL

"*C*ongratulations!" they shouted. A cake made of her favorite flavors, a gift card to a local department store and a bottle of the darkest Bahamian rum they could find. Amelia was not only recently promoted to a lead sales position, but it was also in a city far enough away from her past. Her dad had just passed away and a long-term on-again/off-again relationship finally met its bitter end, so this was a definitive sign from whatever 'Heaven' there was that she needed to make her exit, yet again.

She deeply resented the fact that her moment of glory could not really be shared with anyone significant in her life. At the age of thirty, Amelia She had been single now for three weeks and although she was still so raw from that last fight, those last words, and that last glance, she wanted even more to erase it from her mind! She wanted to replace it with a new smile, a new laugh, or a new good time. She wanted a man. She knew that her friends would tease her about being single for any length of time. After all, they knew that she breezed through breakups by enlisting the help of her favorite vices and before long, would have another male counterpart in her life.

But this time felt different. There was a hollowness that she just couldn't shake. She thought of the times they talked about what life would look like if they were married. How much they made each other laugh and how they bounced back after random quarrels. She would still feel the pang of jealousy rise when her mind would then flip back to the ongoing text messages he was always tending to when he was with her. How his disappearances on Saturday nights were becoming too frequent and the excuses were becoming more impossible to believe. The pit of her stomach churned when she realized that he had been using male enhancers, but their intimate life was just fine. The pieces were all so random, but eventually they fit together in the double life he led. The drugs he was using were not just simple party drugs. They cost a great deal of money. Money, she knew he had, but never spent *on her*. Oh, the lies swirled in her head. She saw his face in her mind, how angry he was when he was finally out of answers to her ongoing questions. How hard that shove was he gave her out his front door. How she fell to the hard concrete and he didn't even flinch. He even smirked. The very thought of his face made her blood run cool. That face she had seen too many times growing up. That same expression of hate, disgust, and deep-rooted rage. Was it true that women like her just gravitate towards hateful and abusive men because that is all they are *used to*? Was she, in fact, just another statistic?

"Amelia! Hey! You *okay*, girl?" her co-worker whispered as she placed her hand on Amelia's shoulder. Eva's voice was normally loud but this time, it rendered a sweet concern that she yearned for—from anybody! She sounded like she *cared* if Amelia was okay. Maybe a little too much, matter of fact. Eva wasn't married or never spoke of having a boyfriend. Eva lived alone and always availed herself to Amelia's midnight crying spells over Jacob. She nodded softly to Eva and fixated her stare at the Bahamian rum. *There*, she thought, *that's where the escape will begin tonight!* She looked down at her watch and there were just another forty-five minutes to go before her shift ended. Amelia's heart raced as she thought of how she could muster up the nerve to ask for a day off tomorrow. After all, she was turning up her responsibility beginning on Monday in her new role. It made sense to her to ask for the next day off as she rode out the momentum of the celebratory praises of those surrounding her. Before she knew it, she was inviting the whole department out for drinks after work! Her boss reluctantly agreed to approve the next day off and had a look of concern in her eyes that

Amelia had never seen before. Assuming she was just being paranoid, Amelia thanked her boss and made her way back to her desk.

As she was walking back to her desk, she caught a glimpse of Eva feverishly text messaging on her phone. When Eva looked up at her, she acted startled and placed her phone in her lap. Sheepishly, she half-smiled at Amelia. *Well, that was an unusual reaction*, Amelia thought to herself, but she didn't have time to stop and explore Eva's actions further. She had an all-nighter awaiting her!

On her way home, Amelia stopped for a pack of smokes. It had been hours since she had heard from Eva and knew that given their strange work relationship, if she didn't spend the evening celebrating with Eva directly, she would receive the third degree come Monday! Nevertheless, she didn't want to accidentally miss her call *just in case* she had to cancel. Eva served a purpose to Amelia's weekend charades and late-night crying spells over the last 'mean thing' Jacob said or did. It remained to be seen if things were to change for Amelia's love life, career, or both if Eva would stick around. The very thought of it made her question if Eva was going to be the only option for friendship she would know. *That thought* made her queasy. Amelia instinctively knew that friendship was not supposed to feel this way.

At that very moment, a text message came through.

Maybe someone saw her social media post about getting the promotion and was checking in on the evening details? Excited, Amelia grabbed her phone and opened the message.

As she looked down at her phone, it felt as if all the air was sucked out of the room! Immediately, she thought it was a cruel joke. Someone was sabotaging her joy once again, and was being vindictive. Someone wanted to be 'funny' and trigger her. Who in the world would be behind this text? Whomever it was left themselves anonymous! The text was sent from a # symbol — no name or number visible. "That coward!" she yelled. The man at the counter of the liquor store looked up at her and asked her, "who are you calling a coward, lady?" Amelia looked up at him and quickly apologized. She grabbed her smokes and a handful of small vodka bottles near the change jar, slamming them on the counter. The man looked up at her, smiled, and shoved them into a bag. He took her ten dollars and gave her back change for the smokes. He then jokingly said, "the bottles are on me so you can forget about the coward!" Amelia locked eyes with him and said, "never. I'll never forget. And, neither will *THEY!*"

Looking down at her phone one more time before putting the keys into the ignition, she let out a guttural growl and drank the first bottle. Then, the second one. Then, the third. The burning in her throat subsided, so she lit a cigarette.

Breathing deeply, she looked up into the fading sunset and whispered softly to *'That Jesus,'* "Hey, it's me again. I guess You may have had something to do with this one. Well, that's okay. You have shown me You are in control and that's all been fun and games until now. I am taking this ride back over, okay? Just turn Your head and let me fix this *my way*! You know what I have been through and if it all hasn't killed me yet, this is the closest I am coming to death. But, on MY terms, okay? Just *BACK OFF, Jesus,* and let me handle this. If You let me live through this and I get away with it, I'll consider letting You back in. But those are my terms. You hear me? *My terms!*"

She flipped the lid off the fourth bottle, drank it, shoved it back into the bag and turned on the ignition. Glancing back over at the phone, the image of Eva sitting on Jacob's motorcycle with his arms wrapped around her waist didn't just provoke anger, it provoked a deep need for revenge that began to consume her as she thought of ways to make both of them regret betraying her. And whomever was texting this picture never included a name, only the picture with a text that read, 'and they are engaged.' The words seemed to jump off the screen!

Amelia transferred all the years of loneliness, humiliation, unrequited love and injustice into a scornful desire to exact revenge on both Eva and Jacob for what they did! She envisioned confronting the two of them when they least expected it. Given her party-girl lifestyle and hot-tempered rampages she was already known for, she wanted both Eva and Jacob to know how deeply she was hurt.

There was still a part of her that wanted Jacob to feel something for her. She wanted him to feel *anything*! What if he apologized and after being publicly humiliated, crawled back to her? Then *he* would be in the same position she had been for years — NOT in control and begging for someone to love him. Surprisingly, her heart became heavy at the very thought of him being in any kind of emotional pain. There was *still* a part of her that loved him. At least what she thought love was supposed to feel like. She never really knew up to this point. She had never experienced unconditional love or respect in a relationship. She certainly didn't have that kind of love with either of her parents or her late brother Bruce, who was too much of 'a taker' to really feel for another person, she thought.

Her heart wandered back and forth from deep despair to hatred! She just wanted it all to stop.

Amelia made it to the bar just in time to meet everyone from work. Oddly, Eva was not there. Hours had passed and Amelia did not even receive a text from her. Knocking back shot after shot, her inner rage was only being fueled by the whiskey. Without saying goodnight to her party friends, she exited the bar and headed downtown to Jacob's favorite hangout. Parking her car only one block from the restaurant, she stumbled into the back patio near the band entrance. Scanning the room for either Jacob or Eva, Amelia was like a lion stalking their prey. Suddenly, she spotted them. Eva and Jacob were sitting at a table with another couple, laughing and holding hands.

"No!" cried Amelia. "No!"

Grabbing Eva by her hair, Amelia began hitting her violently. She tasted blood on her lip as it splashed on her face. Amelia could only hear her own heartbeat getting louder and noticed Eva's grip on her arm loosen. Amelia opened her eyes to see her own blood-soaked hands. Looking up, Jacob's face was the last thing Amelia remembered seeing as everything around her turned to black.

THE SENTENCING

"*A*ll rise," said the court's bailiff.

This was the moment that Amelia had been waiting for. All her years of running from one hot pursuit of love, revenge, justice, and escape from the memories had cumulated to this moment. The drug-induced rages, the drunken blackouts and barefoot walks of shame in the early morning stillness had come to a crushing end. Forcibly, she made the madness stop. One text message two months ago changed the trajectory of her life forever. She never found out who sent that text and her defense attorney didn't care about it. Her request to 'That Jesus' to 'do things her way' and demanding His backing out of her life was granted. She took matters into her own hands. It was her hands that executed her plan of revenge on Eva and Jacob. It was her hands that left the markings on Eva's body that were the proof the jury needed to convict her of aggravated battery, a plea bargain that her attorney arranged. A plea bargain that was another escape from the greater charge of attempted murder that she could have been charged with. She was to be grateful, but she wasn't. If anything, she was numb. She was tired of feeling anything.

The prosecutor spoke of how the fight was initiated by her that night. They brought in witnesses that described Amelia in a 'drunken rage' that night when she entered the restaurant that Eva and Jacob were dining in. Amelia was described as loud, vulgar, and intentional in her attack, dragging Eva out of her chair and beating her mercilessly.

Amelia suddenly screamed, "I didn't mean for her to never be the same! I just wanted to hurt her the way she hurt me! I wanted her to HURT, not end up in a coma!"

The judge slammed the gavel repeatedly as shouts filled the air from Eva's family and Jacob's face was all she could see. His eyes were cold, his face was pale, and his mouth was turned downward. His face was like stone. He sat motionless. She wanted him to know her intention was to shake them both with a public display, but allowing that text to haunt her every thought, she just snapped. She wanted the life that Eva had! She wanted the love that Eva had!

But above anything else, she wanted to lose the feeling of ever wanting to escape again.

Her attorney told her that he was requesting a

restoration program for her behind bars that would shorten her sentence if she would just comply. It would be predicated on the completion of a full detox plan that took the court's mercy to grant. She was on the brink of sabotaging yet another blessing she was receiving and knew she had to keep her mouth shut before she was charged with contempt. Listening to him lecture her oddly brought her comfort. For once in her life, she was being counseled by someone who earnestly cared. Unlike the way she was often left to her own devices, she was being steered by an authority figure. She wondered for a fleeting minute if this is what being loved and guided by God felt like. After all, several of the women she was in holding with struck up a conversation about God with her. They spoke of how they were disobedient and that they were guilty, but God loved them. They mentioned Jesus. They talked about how they knew of His teachings but allowed their flesh to take over. Although several of them were in for violent crimes or grand theft, they spoke of how He still forgives them and will restore them. Amelia listened but chuckled to herself. The thought of restoration was always a fairy tale that the preacher spoke of in that old mountainside chapel. *There was no way*, she thought, that God would forgive her like that. No way at all.

"For the charge of aggravated battery, we the jury, find the defendant guilty."

The words no sooner left the juror's mouth when she

felt relief. She was relieved she didn't have to return to her life she once knew. The life of emptiness, loss, and confusion. She wasn't as sad as she thought she would be. She was instead fearful. She felt scared that she wouldn't survive the detox plan and would never enter the restoration program. What was this feeling that she was experiencing besides fear? Could it be hope?

Her attorney was briefing her, but Amelia couldn't process what he was saying. She just caught a glimpse of Jacob walking out of the courtroom over her attorney's shoulder. He got to the door and hesitated for a few seconds. *Turn around*, Amelia thought. *Turn around!* But, instead, Jacob just walked out the door. Amelia's wish had come true. She had taken charge of the situation and ensured that Jacob would never hurt her again. She also soon realized he would never love her again either.

A FAMILIAR ENCOUNTER

*T*hat afternoon was a blur of processing, lecture, and instruction. She was transported via bus to the state prison two hours away. The guard that was assigned to her was unusually nice. She was telling Amelia all about the detox facility and that she has seen many people come out of it successfully. Amelia listened, but never responded. This new thing, hope, was rearing its head again and like meeting someone new, Amelia studied it carefully to see if it could be trusted.

When they arrived at the facility, the foyer was bright and filled with natural light. There was music playing and it smelled of lavender. Unlike a cold, hard prison program seen in the movies, this one was different. The orderly escorted her and the guard to her room. She was shaking still as it had been only two days since she pulled an all-nighter at home. She was able to post bond with the help of her cousin Lori and put her aunt's house up as collateral. Until the day of the trial, she stayed in her apartment drunk. She wore an ankle monitor, so leaving was not an option. She only chatted on social media with strangers as all of those she once knew stopped talking to her. She felt that she was being prepped for a life of solitude, so her sentencing didn't surprise her.

She didn't sleep much that night, filled with anticipation of what this intake meeting would uncover. Walking in the ankle shackles was worse than five-inch stilettos on ladies' night, but she knew she had to get used to it. The sound of the chains dragging behind her echoed in the hallway. As she walked, she began to hear a faint sound of a crowd shouting. She couldn't make out what the crowd was saying, but she knew they were angry. Her hands began to sweat and looking down at her palms, they were turning red. As she looked up, she began to see an image coming towards her. The doors and floor were blurred by a white mist. She was being drawn into the image. She saw that it was an image of a man. Even though he was still off in a distance from her, she could see his eyes. They were not just *any shade of blue,* they were piercing blue! As this man drew closer, she thought to herself, *isn't anyone else seeing this guy? If so, why is he staring right at me and walking in the middle of the hallway?'*

She suddenly recognized Him. Not a word was

spoken. Not one introduction was needed. Without blinking, she stared into His eyes and *knew* it was Him. It was *'That Jesus!'* She let out a loud cry, "NO!" and in a flash, He was gone.

The guard yanked her arm hard and stepping into her view shouting, "Stop it, prisoner! Stop it right NOW!"

Without another word and what seemed like one big choreographed move, she was being buckled into a chair. Looking out into the hallway, there was no one else standing there and the shouting crowd hushed. Instinctively, she knew that she better not tell anyone, or it could mean a whole new program for her. She thought she must have been hallucinating from the alcohol withdrawals. Either way, she wasn't saying a word to anyone! Glancing down at her palms, they were pale.

"Hello, Amelia," a woman's voice pierced her attention. But this wasn't just any voice. It was familiar. Looking up at the face at the woman, Amelia was certain that her own heart stopped beating! Tears filled her eyes as she sat in front of someone whose disappearance from Amelia's life decades before secretly haunted her. The person who began this routine of escape with her and of all people, *should* understand her. Her teenage friend Denise was the intake counselor.

"You look rough, girl. You look like you've been through it. And I know that you have. But you *chose* to be here a long time ago. I'm going to help you see that and I am going to help you see that there is hope. Hope for a future that has been pre-ordained for you. It will be a future designed to prosper you. Also, all those tears you have cried have come at a price. A price that was already paid. I will teach you about that, too. But you must do one thing before we can begin," she said.

Amelia's voice cracked and she responded, "What's that?"

"You must confess," she said.

Amelia thought she knew what she meant and with a lump in her throat, she dropped her head and began to sob. *"No way, there is NO way I am doing that,"* she thought. *"No way!"*

"Hear what I am saying, Amelia," Denise continued. "Sometimes saying out loud what you did to get here helps the process move along. Hearing the words come out of our own mouths helps us take accountability for what we have done. A confession is needed, for many reasons."

"Who are YOU kidding?" shrieked Amelia. "You were just as horrible a kid as I was and didn't come from anything different than I did! Who are YOU to judge me? *You* left me and never reached back out to me!" Amelia was glaring at Denise at this point and every bit of the confusion she had felt for three decades came flooding back!

"Amelia, I am not in a position to talk about that and it is irrelevant to your case," Denise said sternly. "Besides, I had no control over that period of my life whereas, you, Amelia have always had control. You just chose to make foolish choices with it."

"Oh, now you are sounding like my mom, Nadia! She always liked you and didn't know what a party girl you were. She never knew about us that New Year's Eve. You were just suddenly out of my life and mom was just as confused," she added. "She loved you," whispered Amelia. She felt her eyes well up with tears again.

"And Nadia has been gone how long now?" Denise asked.

Amelia just lowered her head and began to cry. For the first time since her mother's death, she felt her loss. She felt shame and disappointment. And oddly, she felt relief.

SURRENDER & CAPTURE

BY AN UNEXPECTED VISITOR

hree months had passed, and she still had several bouts of rage during her therapy sessions. She thought they were cruelly invasive and brought back a range of emotions that Amelia spent years burying under her vices. Now being ninety days sober, she was able to feel her way through some of her memories. These last ninety days were arduous and her therapist Denise had managed to usher Amelia into a place of transparency about her addictions and face the sobering truths she wanted to deny.

It was a normal Thursday when she was summoned from the recreation room for a visitation notice. She was not expecting anyone. She didn't have anyone from her old circle to rely on and her family was gone. Looking across the room to all the tables she saw that no one was sitting alone. Each table had a guest and a prisoner, so she thought at that moment that someone must be playing a cruel joke on her.

Turning to the guard and stopping in the middle of the entrance to the room, Amelia said. "Listen, I don't have anyone coming to see me and whatever psychological trick Denise is trying on me, she failed. I need to return to my scrabble game. I mean, for once, I am winning!"

Ignoring her, the guard motioned towards the window. There, in one of the two chairs directly in the sunlight was a man in a fedora. She didn't recognize him. The guard gently grabbed her arm and without saying a word, took three giant steps towards the window. When he stopped, he twirled her around and placed her in the seat in front of the man. Just as quickly, the guard resumed his post at the front entrance near the check-in desk.

Amelia noticed immediately that the man, although not a familiar face, had a great smile. His eyes were also familiar. They were a deep, piercing blue, just like 'That Jesus' had in her vision months before.

"Amelia, thank you for meeting with me today, dear. I have been waiting for a long time to come speak to you, so I am so grateful that I could come sit with you face to face. You're so special to me and I can't find the words to let you know how much my heart has hurt watching you go through all of this," he said.

"I'm sorry, who *exactly* are you and how do you know me?" Amelia asked.

"I've always known you," He replied.

"Listen, if you are some creep stalker, I need to warn you. These hands have hurt many and I am not afraid of you or what taking you down will cause. So, cough up your agenda, man and give it to me straight!" she demanded.

Staring into His deep blue eyes made her instantly regret speaking so harshly. She then said, "What I mean is, I am not recognizing you and I have no one else in my life that would travel all this way to see me. So, what is it that you want?"

"Amelia, no matter how hard your life has been up to now, I have always watched you fight," he said softly. "I have known your tears, your fears, your songs you used to sing on the tire swing and how much you loved gardenias! What has hurt you has hurt me."

With tears welling up in her eyes, she was trying to determine if she should be scared for her life right now or if this hallucination was going somewhere.

"Gardenias?" she asked. Her voice quivered as she remembered the box fans in her bedroom window, blowing in that intoxicating fragrance. The corners of her mouth turned up slightly.

"Seriously, *who are you* and why do you know so much about me and my songs? My *own mother* didn't know about those!" Amelia said with a polite authority in her voice.

She looked around her and the guards were not turned

towards her, no one else in that room was even looking in her direction. She knew that between her body language and the volume of her voice, someone would have taken notice by now. The warm rays of the sun were bouncing off her left cheek as she glanced back at him. His face was rugged, but not in an old way. The tone of his voice echoed a deep wisdom. Those eyes seemed to look right through her!

"My dear Amelia. You came so close to feeling My love for you. Remember those girls that were pointing at you at church? They went on to live fulfilling lives of marriage and motherhood. Only after they stopped trying to escape did they live the life I had already arranged for them to have! It took them being in a place of darkness to surrender their lives to Me and become captured by My Spirit," He said.

"It's time, Amelia. Your surrender is needed in order to walk in the call I have for your life, beloved. You weren't meant to be captured into captivity. You were meant to be captured into freedom. And not the kind of freedom that led you to this place. A freedom where you can be loved by Me unconditionally, wholly, and with reckless abandon. Experience freedom from the curses spoken over you so you can find your purpose and live abundantly."

She listened to His promises, His observations of her life, and His direction. He was always there! He gave her every detail of her life. She denied Him access into her heart for years and now the feeling in her heart was a new one. It was being filled with hope. She knew this feeling was also love.

She knew at that moment her years of chasing the next great escape had come to an end. Just like her dad would always tell her that one day, she will come face to face with 'That Jesus' and answer for herself. She just never envisioned that He would be in a fedora, visiting her on a Thursday.

"So, you are Jesus? And I am not dead, nor am I in Heaven. There are no clouds at my feet, and I didn't see an angel on the way into this room. But *you* are Jesus?" she retorted.

"Yes, I am *That* Jesus," He replied, with a slight smirk.

"Okay, then," Amelia said. "Capture me."

"Surrender," He responded. "Stop escaping Me and surrender. Allow My Spirit to truly capture you!"

Bowing her head, she began to sob uncontrollably. As the rays of sunlight faded and there were no other distant conversations overheard, she decided to ask Him what else He wanted from her.

But, to her amazement, He was gone.

LOVE NEVER FAILS: THE BOOK OF FAITH

ROUNDTREE MONTFORD

&

DH BONNER

"And now abideth faith, hope, charity, these three;
but the greatest of these is charity."
~1 Corinthians 13:13

PROLOGUE

Tera moved effortlessly toward the courtyard. With its meticulously manicured lawn, it was breathtakingly beautiful, filled with rows of palm, sycamore, and fruit trees whose limbs were always bending under the weight of their succulent offerings. Pulling down a handful of fruit from one of the trees, Tera stopped and put some in her pocket.

She then closed her eyes and brought a sample to her mouth, indulging in the sweet, honey delicacy that was always perfect in color, texture, and taste — no matter the season. Resting momentarily on a bench honed of jasper and ivory, Tera paused and allowed all of her senses to be engaged in a most wonderful experience.

Taking in the beauty and fragrance of the brilliantly colored flowers swaying in the gentle breeze, she shut her eyes again and felt an almost indescribable euphoric rush as this same breeze gently caressed her skin while depositing a fine mist of perfume it has freed from the surrounding flowers in the courtyard garden.

Tera silently enjoyed the companionship of the slight wind stirring about her as it lovingly serenaded her with whispers of melodious songs echoed from the birds singing off in the distance.

As she embraced the perfect mixture of the warmth of the sun and the coolness of the breeze, Tera felt as if both seemed to be purposefully lingering this morning just to escort her on this journey. So, chaperoned by the two celestial elements, she followed the path of the winding walkway that carried her past the exquisitely sculptured fountains with their cascading waterfalls, to the outer perimeter of the courtyard, and then beyond the playgrounds perched on the hilltops that mirrored one another on either side.

After spending a few unhurried minutes taking in the picturesque view of the valley from her vantage point on the plateau, Tera breathed deeply, held it for what seemed an eternity, and then slowly exhaled; not wanting to miss anything. But she knew that she shouldn't linger too much longer, or she would miss the highlight of her morning; therefore, she began to make her way down to a small trail nestled between two rows of tall, flowering magnolia trees.

This path then brought her to a rustic little arched bridge, intricately carved of cedar, which allowed her to cross over a lazy, babbling brook. From here, Tera could see one of her favorite spots in a quiet little grove tucked in the shade of a cluster of massive oaks trees, which was near the outer corner of an open field full of lavender wildflowers that grew well beyond her sight. As if lifted by the energy of the sun, and carried by the wind, she danced her way through the field of lavender, spinning and leaping like a poised ballerina performing a mesmerizing waltz.

Once she reached her destination, she graciously acknowledged her invisible audience by taking a grand bow and blowing several kisses into the wind.

Giggling with delight at the joy that bubbled within her, she finally collapsed onto the lush green carpet of grass, placed the fruit that remained from what she'd picked earlier in a safe place under one of the trees, and rolled over onto her back.

At that moment, a high-pitched squeal of glee from a playground on one of the twin hilltops pierced the air and immediately filled the atmosphere with youthful joy. Tera didn't even have to look to know exactly who it was.

Sasha entered into the play area, shrieking with delight and appearing to be bounding like a gazelle rather than skipping through the garden. Through half-closed eyelids, Tera watched as one of the Guardians gently motioned for Sasha to lower her voice just a little and to stop running over the other cherubs playing there. She chuckled to herself. Any attempt to try and monitor her playmate's movements would only prove to be a lesson in futility, as keeping up with her was like trying to trace the path of a lightning bolt! And, to confirm her thought, as soon as Sasha passed the Guardian, she sung out a lyrical 'hello,' using the hilltops as background singers to echo the harmonies, and took off in a sprint toward Tera.

Although Tera had only come into the area a short time earlier, it was as if she and Sasha had known each other from the beginning of time.

The two playmates had been inseparable since the first moment they sat beside each other in class. It was amazing how intrinsically they had bonded; they were like two puzzle pieces that fit perfectly together. They finished each other's thoughts and sentences with absolutely no effort at all. They laughed at all the same things... cried at the same things. They both loved music, the sounds of the ocean, hopscotch, butterflies, and butterscotch fudge. It was as if they shared the same heart and mind.

Since they'd been together, the rhythm of their breathing had become synchronized, and even their heartbeats seemed to function as one.

They just flowed that way.

However, there were a couple of things noticeably different about them. While Sasha was like a brilliant flash of energy that never seemed to pause for more than a few seconds, Tera, on the other hand, was quite laid back and relaxed. More like the soothing, flickering flame of a candle. Where Sasha was highly conceptual and able to quickly perceive broad strokes on a large canvas, Tera was very meticulous, paying close attention to every detail. Nevertheless, they seemed to balance each other out perfectly.

They were best friends in every sense of the word.

The atmosphere became increasingly charged with joviality, announcing the approaching presence of her friend's spirit. Yet, before she could completely open her eyes, she was already being bombarded with tickles and kisses and cheerful giggles and chatter from Sasha... essentially senseless to resist. And truth be told, Tera had no desire to. As always, she was thrilled to see her best friend - and this was evident by the shrill of laughter that erupted from within her—completely unhindered.

Tera pretended to resist Sasha's affectionate attack, but quickly threw her hands up and fell back in total surrender. They both giggled uncontrollably with tears of joy flowing freely as Sasha fluttered about with her arms raised, performing a silly little dance in recognition of yet another victorious win.

They were both super excited about today's meeting because it was a celebration of sorts. They had reached the close of this school session, and they had both done exceptionally well. Although Tera had transferred late into the term, she had worked diligently to catch up. She had turned in her final lesson yesterday and was awaiting that grade. Provided she passed that one, she could move on to the special "field assignment."

Sasha had received a passing grade on all of her lessons, and the only thing that stood between her and a promotion was the field assignment. Her invitation to the Throne Room was delivered by special messenger from the King Himself, and after sharing the news with her parents, she had raced over, invitation in hand, to share this news with Tera.

Upon removing an ivory-colored piece of paper from the gold-rimmed envelope bearing the King's official seal and placing it into her friend's hand, Sasha watched closely as Tera read the calligraphic lettering that congratulated Sasha on the successful completion of her training and provided initial instructions to report to a specified Guardian who was the Keeper of the Books, for there she would choose her assignment and be given further instruction.

The last detail on the invitation stated that she should come prepared to be on field assignment for an indeterminate length of time. With this in mind, Sasha and Tera decided to make this playdate really special; such would be their adventure today.

As Sasha took a moment to rest after her victory dance, Tera retrieved the fruit that she had placed in the shade of the other tree and was returning to join Sasha.

Sasha, whose curiosity had gotten the better of her,

was already approaching Tera with an inquisitive look on her face. Tera smiled and extended her offering of fruit to her friend; Sasha squealed and graciously accepted.

With one hand, she tucked the fruit in her pocket, and with the other, she gently took Tera by the hand. Without ever exchanging a word, they both began to run full throttle across the field. As if being energized by their connection, they were lifted by the wind and began to soar toward the fluffy white clouds and the bright sun that decorated the radiant blue sky.

As they released each other's grip, their bodies seem to transform into a lighter, almost translucent form. They soared in complete synchronization, first in parallel waves and loops, and then in alternating zig-zag patterns, floating over peaks and valleys, and leaving the field far behind in the distance.

Dipping downward toward the dense green thicket, they slowed long enough to flutter with the butterflies as they flitted about. Then, increasing their speed, they rode the rush of cascading waterfalls and sailed just above the white water as it raced toward another fall.

They smiled and greeted other kingdom citizens who were using the same mode of travel, and using the power of the wind, mimicked the majestic maneuvers of a lone eagle that occasionally crossed their path.

Even though they had not discussed their destination, it was as if they instinctively knew where they were going.

Just as they came upon the sparkling white sand and crystal-clear water, the two cherubs began to descend.

The beach was bustling with activity—from those sunbathing, or tossing frisbees or playing volleyball, to those frolicking at the shoreline, or those sailing and speedboating. Tera and Sasha walked the shoreline until they found a suitable spot and then settled in to enjoy a snack. It didn't take long for them to make friends with other cherubs, and together they engaged in delightful play for hours on end.

Realizing that the sun, who had been their constant companion, was now drifting away toward the horizon, they decided it was time to return home. They followed the reverse path back, flying over the lavender field, past the playgrounds, and landing in the courtyard just outside the Hall of Learning.

It was now almost dusk, and they knew that it was time to part ways. Although Tera knew she would not be allowed into the Throne Room during Sasha's session the next day, she promised that she would meet her in the north courtyard adjacent to the King's palace and escort her to the Guardian's desk.

Bright and early the following morning, they met at the designated place. Even though Sasha was her usual exuberant self, she seemed a little quieter today. Sensing the concern in her friend's spirit, Tera assured her that all was well and took a moment to pray with Sasha before they entered the palace:

> Dear Righteous King of Kings, we humbly ask that you would endow Sasha with the wisdom to choose the right assignment and give her the influence to alter the course of their eternal destiny by drawing them to you so that they may become a citizen of your glorious Kingdom; and in so doing, that Sasha may gain her angel wings.
>
> Thank you, Lord... Amen.

Sasha exuberantly echoed Tera's amen, and then the two friends followed the map printed on the reverse of Sasha's invitation. The Palace was massive and full of countless hallways and levels, so the map and the door plaques were invaluable. Sasha was genuinely grateful that her bestie had accompanied her.

As they reached the top of the flight of crystal stairs, there was a massive set of double doors and a golden plaque with diamond lettering that read "THRONE ROOM" where Guardians were stationed on either side of the entrance. Sasha and Tera exchanged a holy kiss and shared a lingering embrace; then, Tera took a seat on the far end of the top step as Sasha presented her invitation to the Guardian closest to her.

A chime rang, the double doors opened, and the Guardian silently pointed Sasha to an office on the right, just inside the massive hall.

Glancing over at her cherubic sister-friend, Sasha nervously smiled, and upon seeing Tera lovingly smiling back at her, she proceeded as directed, as the doors slowly closed behind her.

At that moment, Tera felt as if she could instantly transform from a flickering light into a massive ball of intense energy because she was so overwhelmed with joy for her friend. When she stood up to leave the palace and return to the courtyard, a second chime rang, and the doors to the Throne Room opened once again.

Was there something amiss? Had Sasha forgotten something? Was her assignment complete so soon? What was happening?

This time, however, the Guardian motioned for Tera to come forward. With great anticipation and humility, she approached him, awaiting news. In silence, he handed her a gold-rimmed envelope, bearing the King's official seal. . . with her name on it.

She had completed her last lesson with flying colors and was now receiving her invitation to select her field assignment.

MOVING

The alarm on Cassie's cellphone was ringing through her subconscious. It took her a moment to understand why the continual tinkling in the distance wasn't mixing well with the giggles and laughter in her dream and even a few minutes more to become conscious enough to locate the dismiss button on her device and shut it off.

She only managed to hit snooze.

Never opening her eyes, Cassie turned back over, pulled the covers over her head, and tried to find her way back into the dream. After what seemed like just a few seconds, the alarm went off again.

"Cassie. Get up..." her mom said, as she crossed the room to the nightstand next to Cassie's bed and gently turned off the alarm.

Cassie mumbled something incoherent, serving only to provoke her mother.

"I said NOW, Cassie!"

Knowing better than to respond disrespectfully or to push further, Cassie stuck her feet outside the bedspread and slowly planted them on the floor — first one, then the other. The rest of her body followed shortly, her head emerging last. As she stood to full height, she found herself face to face with her mother.

Well... chin to the top of her head, to be more exact.

Her mom was a heavyset 5′2″, and with Cassie at just a couple of inches shy of six feet, she had definitely taken her height from her father's side of the family. However, her height was about all she inherited from her father in terms of looks, because like her mom, her mother's mom, and her mother's sisters and aunts, she too was full-figured. She had also inherited her mother's deeply melanated skin and hazel colored eyes.

So, besides the slightly more than half-foot difference, the two were practically mirror images of one another.

"Good morning," her mother said with a stern look, yet still reaching up and kissing her daughter on the cheek. "I need you up and at 'em dear. Like I told you and your brother last night, we've got a lot to do today."

"Good morning, Mom. I'm sorry. I'll get washed up and be right down."

"Fine. You'll have to grab cereal for breakfast today.

There's not much in the fridge, and I'm not going to the store to buy food that we'll just be throwing away in another day or two."

Cassie nodded. "Not a problem. I'm not that hungry right now anyway," she replied, throwing on the sweatpants and t-shirt she had placed on the foot of the bed the night before, untying her headscarf as she made her way to the bathroom.

Her mother followed closely behind, making sure that Cassie didn't somehow make her way back into the bed. This didn't go unnoticed by Cassie, but she didn't want to create any more issues than were already on the table. As she closed the bathroom door behind her and heard her mom's footsteps going down the stairs to the first floor of the house, Cassie let out a deep sigh and turned on the faucet in the sink to mask the sound of her spoken prayer, "Father God, thank You for this day You have made. I will be exceedingly, abundantly, and over joyously glad in it. Thank You for Your manifold blessings and for keeping me... in spite of me. Thank You for grace that abounds and for mercies that endure forever. I am thankful."

After reciting her morning prayer by rote, Cassie took hold of her toothbrush, placed the paste onto it, and stared into her mirrored reflection. She continued, "But, I'm really not too happy about this move, and I'm not sure why You haven't done anything to stop it. This is crazy, and you know it!"

As she brushed her teeth, the tears slowly began to flow down her face. Cassie decided not to do anything to stop them. She had been overwhelmed with what she felt was the unfairness of it all, and try as she might to be okay with things, it had become a source of tension between her and her parents.

It wasn't moving in general that bothered her so much. As a "GI Brat," she was used to moving. In her 17 years of life, she had lived in various countries spanning four different continents. The problem was with this particular move. She had already attended two high schools in the past three years and was preparing to enter her senior year in the fall.

Now, since her father was retiring after 20 years of military service, they were moving to Central Florida, where both of her parent's families were.

But, this was her senior year! She would be starting all over again and graduating with people she didn't even know. What about her chair position in music? What about her ranking in academics? What about prom?

Cassie had even asked if she could stay with close friends for the next school year, a family she knew her parents trusted, but they quickly said no, leading to a heated discussion and leaving behind hurt feelings.

Hers... not theirs.

At one point in the disagreement, her younger brother, Jayson, tried to interject that it wasn't bothering him, so why should it bother her, which prompted some not so choice words being hurled at him with the intent being to destroy him — as only an older sibling can.

Cassie quipped that it didn't bother him because he never had any friends to lose anyway, which, of course, was not true. It was just that there was a four-year difference between the two of them, and Jayson would be starting his freshman year; and with their father being retired, the moving would stop, so he would be able to grow up with this same group of kids. Cassie knew that she was envious of him for this reason, but she wasn't going to tell him that.

Instead, she called him a sorry loser, he responded by calling her a fat, ugly heifer. It escalated and quickly went downhill from there, ending only after her mother screamed "enough!" at the top of her lungs.

Rinsing the washcloth under the warm stream of water flowing from the faucet, Cassie wiped her face, removing all trace of tears. After placing her toothbrush back into the holder and putting her towel back on the rack to air dry, she combed her hair out, applied some mascara to her lashes, and dabbed a bit of Vaseline on her lips.

Opening the bathroom door, she went downstairs to join the rest of her family.

MEMORIES

*I*t was the first day of my senior year in high school. I had gotten to the bus stop at least half an hour before any of the other kids, sat down on the bench, and set my bookbag beside me to make sure that no one could sit in that space. For now, it was quiet, and I liked it that way. I just did not have the energy or desire to engage in juvenile chit chat with anyone.

Over the past decade, my feigned smile and soft words had hidden the volcano of emotions that was on the brink of eruption; so, my melancholy was merely the crescendo to a symphony of pain and anguish whose composition began long ago — and that today was resonating ever so loudly.

As I sat on the bench at the corner bus stop, apprehensive and anxious about how I was going to get through this day, let alone another year, the memory once again flooded my soul.

I was about seven or eight years old and bubbling with excitement because we had Friday off from school, and I was going to spend all three days at my cousin Imani's house.

Me and Mani, as she was affectionately called, had been having secret "G-14 classified" undercover meetings every time our families got together. We would escape to the privacy of the big shade tree in my front yard so we could work on a plan to convince our parents to let us spend this weekend together but trick them into thinking that the whole thing was their idea. The plan apparently worked because Mama dropped me off at Aunt Belle and Uncle George's house early that Friday morning.

Mani and I had planned every detail of our weekend together, including which outfits we would wear each day, what we would do, and which neighbors we would play with. I was so excited that I had packed my clothes in a brown paper bag on Tuesday and tucked it away in my closet. I was up bright and early that Friday morning — I quickly dressed in the designated outfit of the day, brushed my teeth, combed my hair, and packed another bag with all my favorite toys. I sat both bags on the front porch near the door and perched myself on the top step, anxiously waiting for Mama to come out.

I could hear her barking out final orders to my

brothers, followed by a verbal prayer, as she exited the door, "And I betta not find da whole neighborhood in my house when I get home! Jeezus p l e a s e let dez knuckle-headed boys not try me ta-day!"

The burrows in her forehead softened as she surveyed my "luggage." She laughed and said, "My Lord child, you think you got enough stuff? You're only going for the weekend; you're not moving away!"

I gave her a sheepish smile, as I secretly prayed that she would not make me leave any of my precious cargo.

As we made our way to the car, her monologue continued... "How is it that I have to fuss and threaten you and your brothers, and practically drag y'all outta bed on school days, but you can get up today with no problem?" Although I saw her lips moving, I couldn't tell you anything else she said because my mind was busy going over the weekend itinerary that Mani and I had planned.

"Trinity Elise Jones...did you hear what I said?! You better be on your best behavior. Don't let me hear a bad report about you."

"Yes, Ma'am, Mama. I will."

As the car stopped in the driveway, Mani was sitting on the front steps anxiously awaiting our arrival. We both ran to greet each other with giggles and hugs. We mumbled a quick greeting to our respective aunties as we each grabbed a bag from the backseat of the car and scurried off.

Mani and I had a glorious day of carefree play... No

fancy toys or trips to a theme park — just simple children's play fueled only by our rich imaginations. We played outside in the summer heat with the neighborhood kids, pretending to be everything from Cowboys and Indians, to mommies with babies, strollers and baby bottles, to beautiful princesses — complete with fire-breathing dragons and knights in shining armor (played by some of the neighborhood boys who were too small to be involved in the football scrimmage going on in the open field across the street).

We played intermittently with most of the children within a two-three street radius, but mainly with Faith and Hope, the Johnson twins who lived in the red brick house on the corner. We went from make-believe to hopscotch, and then from hopscotch to double-dutch, and finally, to skating and bicycle riding.

We gladly took turns cooling off by drinking the lukewarm water from Mrs. Johnson's garden hose after riding Faith and Hope's bicycles, or after being pulled like a caboose on our Union 5 skates by the same rope we'd used to jump with earlier, that was now tied to the back of their bicycles. We even got a special treat from Mrs. Johnson after the crowd thinned out - Me and Mani, and Faith and Hope each got our very own popsicle (not just a half of one that I was accustomed to getting at home).

We laughed and played until the sun had set and disappeared behind the houses off in the distance, and the street lights came on, and until we heard Aunt Belle holler our names from the front steps, saying that supper was ready and that it was time to come inside. After making plans to meet again the next day, we said goodbye to Faith and Hope, and then Mani and I raced each other down the block as if we were running the last leg of an Olympic relay race.

After supper, we helped clean the kitchen — Mani washed the dishes, and I dried them — and together, we put them away. Aunt Belle inspected our work before she swept and mopped the kitchen floor.

As we washed away the gritty reward of a rich day of play, we giggled and whispered in the bathtub about how our ingenious plan had come together. Our bath towels magically transformed us into movie stars as they instantly became either beautiful flowing hair or an elegant evening gown, and the toothbrush became the microphone that we used to address our adoring fans. We pranced and twirled and blew kisses as we graced the imaginary red carpet. We were content to stay in our make-believe world until my cousin Jacob (Mani's brother) started banging on the bathroom door.

"How long y'all gon be in there? Mama, they still in there playin'!"

Clad only in t-shirt and panties, we licked our tongues as we bolted past Jacob in the hallway.

"Y'all betta hurry up and get in that bed!" Aunt Belle

yelled from the front room. "And don't forget to say your prayers!"

"Yes, Ma'am," we replied in perfect unison.

After Mani and I said our prayers, I crawled into the extra twin bed. I drifted off to sleep to the rhythmic humming of the noisy box fan perched on the dresser that was circulating the hot summer night air. Despite the heat, I was smiling as I thought about how much fun we'd had that day. The last thing I remember thinking was how perfect Mani's life was — nice parents that never fought, one brother instead of three, and a beautiful princess room with frilly curtains and two canopy beds and lots of toys... how I wished I were her.

And then, I felt a hand on my mouth.

NEWNESS

*T*he move had gone well, and Cassie's family was settling in just fine. Their new home in Lakeland, a Florida city, centrally located to the west of Orlando and east of Tampa, was a two-story brick townhouse situated right next to a large community park, with only a thin strip of dirt and grass separating the two addresses. Although her parents had decided not to purchase a larger home, since they knew Cassie would be going off to college in another year, there was plenty of space for the four of them, with its three bedrooms, two and a half bathrooms, living room, dining room, and completely built out basement.

This was a home that Cassie had visited many times before. Whenever her father had been sent on a short assignment where the rest of the family couldn't go, they would come and live here with her grandparents. So, she felt extremely comfortable in this house and knew where everything was — every nook and cranny — including the secret place in her bedroom closet. This was why, when given the first pick of the two smaller rooms, she quickly selected the one in the back and furthest from the stairs.

Jayson had just shrugged and trotted off to throw his bag onto the floor in the adjacent room and ran back down the stairs and out the door to begin exploring the neighborhood. He didn't care which room he slept in. He planned to be on the go, making friends and playing ball anyway. But Jayson might have put up a bit more of a fuss had he known about the room's added amenity.

Cassie wasn't going to share that little tidbit. Instead, she put her suitcase and backpack down on the floor at the foot of her bed, closed the door of her room, and then went into the closet. As the large walk-in closet was empty, the thin outline of a second door at the back wall was clearly visible. If the closet had been filled with the usual clothes, shoes, and other personal stuff, you wouldn't have even known it was there.

There was no doorknob or handle on the door, just the outline. But Cassie knew how to open it. It had a spring hinge that only needed a gentle push on the right spot, and it would pop right open.

Cassie walked over to the door, found the sweet spot after a couple of tries, and was delighted when she felt it give way under her fingertips. Stepping inside of the room, she almost bumped her head on the ceiling — the space was not the same height as the closet, and she had grown quite a bit since the last time she had been here — so she had to hunch down slightly.

Pulling on the string that turned on the overhead light, she was surprised that the bulb immediately came on, brightening the space. After all this time, the bulb still works, Cassie thought to herself. No one else had been in here since the last time I was in here? Sitting on the floor of the room, she began to look around and reminisce about the times she had played dolls, made drawings, and wrote letters and songs in this secret place. She had come in here when it was raining, when she was sad, when she felt alone, or merely needed some space to breathe, to think... to be.

She ran her hand across the back wall and felt the lettering she had carved in the wood so many years ago, "CJH" — her initials. Her name, Cassia Janette Hendrickson — and opened the green military footlocker her dad had given her to keep her keepsakes. So many memories. So many countries. So many friends. And, now it was over. It felt like forever, and at the same time, it felt like just yesterday.

After closing the footlocker's lid, Cassie spoke a quiet prayer of thanks to God, turned off the light, and closed the door of the secret room. She was home.

Cassie then spent the next few days emptying boxes —

alternating between emptying the boxes in her room and emptying boxes in any room her mom asked her to. One day, she might have been emptying boxes in the living room, then the next day, it was emptying boxes of kitchen stuff, and on another day, she was emptying boxes in the hallway and putting away odds and ends, sheets, blankets, and towels in hall closets. Cassie didn't mind. There was nothing else she was going to be doing, no one she was going to see, and nowhere else she had plans to be. She was in a new place, albeit a familiar one; she didn't really know anyone or have any close friends she could hang out with... yet.

Lakeland wasn't a big city, as big cities go. It wasn't anything like a Chicago or an Atlanta or a New York. But, as part of Polk County, it was a large enough city, with over thirty beautiful lakes (hence the name Lake-land), an easy drive to a metropolitan area, and within an hour to a beach somewhere.

Ah, the beaches. Cassie hadn't set her toes in the sand in several years, since having just come back stateside from Bitburg, Germany. Although she had gotten the opportunity to visit the Cathedrals in Koln, ride on the Rhine river, stand under the Eiffel tower, and walk along the River Thames after having gazed upon the Big Ben clock tower and the gates of Buckingham Palace, most of her time was spent living on the Air Force Base.

Which made sense, since she was too young to just

walk on and off base without a guardian. However, she gleefully remembered that time when she and a few friends hopped the fence at the back of the military housing area and discovered a farm down the road, complete with a barn and hay bales. Some of the hay hadn't been gathered up yet, so they jumped from off the roof of the barn into the hay, screaming and squealing until the property owners ran them off.

"Mom!" Cassie yelled out suddenly.

In a matter of mere seconds, her mother appeared in the doorway. "Yessss...?"

"Can we go to the beach this weekend?"

"Girl, it's the middle of summer. Do you know how packed North Beach or Clearwater is during this time of year?" Mom asked.

"Well, what about Vero? We haven't been there since I was about seven or eight years old."

"Hmmm... I'll talk to your dad about it later. Maybe we can find a weekly rental right on the beach through Airbnb. That way, we won't have to do a lot of driving or trying to find a parking spot while we're there. We'll see."

Cassia grinned. It didn't come close to making up for the sadness of this move, but it at least gave her something fun to look forward to.

"In the meantime, go empty the boxes in the bathroom," her mother said, as she walked away, her voice breaking into Cassia's happy thoughts.

"As if I haven't emptied enough boxes..." Cassia mumbled under her breath to no one.

"What did you say?"

"Nothing," she replied, standing up and going into the bathroom to continue unpacking.

MONSTERS

Sometime during the dead of night and under cover of darkness, as that one large, strong hand covered my mouth, I felt another hand groping down my t-shirt and then inside my panties. I fought with all my strength, but my fight proved futile against the weight and power of this stranger who was now on top of me. I struggled to scream but couldn't. I was trying to piece together what was happening. Who is this monster hurting me? Where is Mani? Maybe she had gotten away and gone to get help? I strained to try and see her bed, but I could not move.

I tried to scream for help, but my muffled screams went unheard. I vividly recall the total fear and disbelief when the liquor-laced voice whispered his foul threats in my ear, "shhh... you betta not tell nobody or they will say you're a lying, nasty lil girl and they will take you away from your family." So, I lay there in pain and shock as this monster ravaged my innocence and purity.

After a while, I wasn't sure whether I was dead or alive because all of a sudden, there was no longer any pain — all I remember was there was this bright light. Then I was dancing in this open field of wildflowers, and I heard the laughter of children playing and the sound of birds chirping in the trees.

I decided to stay in that beautiful, peaceful place until the monster finished his vile act and slithered out of the room the same way he had entered. I remember looking down and seeing Mani asleep and unharmed in her bed and thinking I need to rescue her before the monster gets her. Then, I saw myself slowly floating back down through the bedroom ceiling and re-entering my own body that was curled up in the other bed. At that very instant, all the pain returned.

Whimpering, I got up and went into the bathroom. I cleaned myself up, stumbled back into Mani's room, and got fully dressed. There in the darkness, I curled up in a ball and lay down at the foot of Mani's bed. I was terrified to close my eyes, so I lay there awake, waiting for morning to come and praying that the monster did not return.

The next morning, I was extremely quiet, still filled with fear and pain — both physically and emotionally; I pretended to be half-asleep as I joined Aunt Belle, Mani, and Jacob in the kitchen. Aunt Belle was cooking breakfast, and Mani and Jacob were sitting at the table. Although Uncle George was not present yet, my senses were on full alert.

"Good morning, Pastor Simpkins. Breakfast will be ready in a minute," Aunt Belle chirped.

"Good morning, my first lady. Thank you, my love," Uncle George responded as he entered the kitchen and took his seat at the head of the table.

Uncle George was burrowing holes into my soul with his intense stare. The same monster who had robbed me of my innocence, who had stolen the sparkle of my purity, was sitting across the table from me, holding my life ransom in exchange for my silence.

"Good morning children, how is everyone this morning?"

"Good morning, Daddy. I'm good!" Imani replied joyfully.

"That's great, princess... I can see that. Good morning Trinity."

Although I had not eaten breakfast yet, I felt myself becoming nauseous and bolted from the table and into the bathroom just in time.

Aunt Belle appeared at the bathroom door shortly after that and offered to fix me some hot tea and asked if I wanted to go back to bed, but I began to cry and insisted that my stomach was hurting, and all I wanted to do was go home.

As I gathered my already packed things, I heard her on the phone with Aaron, my oldest brother. "Okay, well... tell her Trini is not feeling well and wants to come home. Ask her if she wants your Uncle to bring her home, or does she want to come pick her up since she's headed out anyway?" Then, after a short pause, "Okay, I'll let her know she's on the way."

I posted myself on the front steps until my ride arrived. Mani came and sat with me and began to chatter about something, but I had no interest in indulging her in conversation or play. I had one thing on my agenda. . . going home!

Once Mom arrived, I practically scrambled into the car before it had even come to a complete stop. Aaron had come with her, and after Mama had taken a few moments to speak with Aunt Belle, she put the car back into drive, and we left.

"Hey, sugah-lump. How you feeling?"

With tear-filled eyes, I whimpered, "I wanna go home."

I rode the remainder of the trip home in complete silence, curled up in the back seat with my head in Aaron's lap, who had joined me in the back when I got in. He never said a word... he just laid his arm gently over me like a shield.

When we got home, I made my way to my room. Even though it was not nearly as pretty as Mani's, it was a welcomed sight, and it was a safe place. I dug my panties and t-shirt from the bottom of the bag and washed them out in the bathroom sink; then, I hid them in my closet to dry. I sat on the back step and listened to the children playing next door.

As I sat there, it began to rain. My tears mixed with the raindrops that raced down my face, and I prayed that the rain would somehow wash away the pain and confusion — that it would cleanse me of this heavy, dirty cloak of invisible filth and guilt that seemed to be suffocating me.

Sitting there in the rain, I tried to figure out what, if anything, an eight-year-old could do against a monster. Would anyone even believe me, or would they just snatch me up and put me with all the other nasty little girls. Someplace where I would never see Mani, or my parents, or my brothers again. I wondered if there was any reason to even pray about this since the monster worked in God's house. What kind of God would hire monsters to work for Him?

The sound of Mama's voice startled me as her tone laced with annoyance beckoned me back inside, scolding me for sitting outside unprotected in the rain. I thought to myself, "the rain won't hurt me...it's the monster that I need to be protected from."

After changing into dry clothes, I went to Mama and Daddy's room and curled up in their bed. I was looking for a safe place from this awful thing...this secret that I felt like I could never tell anyone. Feeling the safety of being home,

I drifted off to sleep to the sounds of my brother's laughter, and the familiar fragrance of Dial soap, and Shower to Shower talc that graced my parent's linen.

Suddenly, I was jolted back to the present by the voices of other kids coming to the bus stop, which felt like an assault to my ears, and then the sound of the most pleasant voice I had heard in a long time... her words almost melodic.

"Hi! Can I sit here?"

FRIENDS

*I*t was the eve of the first day of school, and although Jayson was so ready for the start of his freshman year — fresh haircut, gear pressed and laid out on the chair in his room with matching kicks, and a cross-body book satchel (he felt he was too old for the standard bookbag) resting by the front door — Cassie was nowhere near prepared for the beginning of her last year of high school.

She wasn't one to sulk, usually... and tonight was no different. However, she was much less cheerful or pleasant than normal. Her mom had given her money to buy new school clothes and supplies, but it still sat on her dresser in the same envelope her mother had handed her. She would be fine wearing what she already had in dresser drawers, and there was nothing wrong with the bookbag she had from last year.

It wasn't that she was afraid about the new school and meeting new kids; she was used to that. As a GI Brat, she had grown up living all over the world, so she was not timid about new places, new faces, or new relationships.

It was that she was unhappy about this particular move, and try as she might, she couldn't shake the feeling of being slighted, that she was missing something special that was supposed to be part of her life. The kids that she would meet this year had already spent their entire elementary and high school years together; they would have formed friendships and groups. She would be an outsider. A stranger. The odd man out. And before she would have a chance to find her place, it would be time to graduate.

All of this made her sad, so she went downstairs to make some popcorn and grab a soda. While she waited for the air popper to heat the kernels, she pulled her cell phone out of her back pocket, and a wave of nostalgia flooded over her. Opening her Facebook app, she scrolled down her feed, checking out what her buddies were doing and talking about, making sure to click the love button or leave a "heart" emoji on her friends' posts to let them know she saw it.

"Don't burn that popcorn, girl! her dad yelled from the front room. "I can't stand that burnt smell... and it takes forever to get it out of the house."

"I won't," Cassie responded. She always waited until

there was a two-three second lag between pops to turn it off. Popcorn was her thing; she wasn't going to burn it.

After adding some popcorn seasoning salt to the bowl, shaking it up, and then adding some more, she grabbed a Mountain Dew from the refrigerator and began walking back to her room.

"You okay, dear?" her mom asked as she passed the living room.

Her mom and dad were cuddled up on the couch, watching a movie. Cassie remembered unpacking the box that held all of the DVDs and putting them away. "Yes, Ma'am. I'm fine."

"Alright. Don't stay up too late. You don't want to miss the bus on your first day of school."

It took everything Cassie had within her not to make a smart retort; she would lose that battle with a quickness. So, instead, she just said, "Yes, Ma'am. Goodnight."

"Goodnight, Baby. See you in the morning..." her mom began, and then her dad joined in, "... Good Lord, willin', and the creek don't rise..."

Cassie muttered the ending of their family's usual nightly saying along with her parents, "...and there's no hole in the boat," as she continued down the hallway and into her room, where she shut the door and stretched out on her bed to eat her popcorn and read a good book before shutting down for the night.

* * *

Cassie awoke the next morning ahead of her cell's reminder and well before the sun had come up. The house was exceptionally quiet; no one else was up yet. She wasn't overly excited or anxious about the day, so why was she awake so early?

As she tightly closed her eyes, buried her face in the pillows, and pulled the covers over her head in an attempt to drop back to sleep, she sensed a strong yet gentle urge to get out of bed and go into the room in the closet. After wrestling with the thought for a few minutes, she swung her legs over the side of the bed, slid her feet into her house shoes, and found her way in the dark to the closet.

Opening the door and turning on the light, Cassie had to blink a few times due to extreme brightness. Quickly though, she was able to see clearly and immediately went to the footlocker and sat down on it.

There was nothing but the emptiness of the small, dank room and deafening silence for a few short minutes. The birds hadn't even gotten up yet to fill the air with their chirping. But soon, Cassie felt the need... no, an overwhelming desire to sing. So, that's what she did.

She sang songs learned in school chorus, she sang songs learned in Sunday school, she sang songs heard on Christian radio, and she even sang a Disney tune that just felt right in the moment. And then she sang a song she had never heard before... anywhere; it seemed to have been downloaded into her heart and burst through her soul. This was a new song — a song that talked about how she was a newcomer in a strange land and had no friends here. But the song was also hopeful because it spoke to how she knew God was with her... that He would never leave or forsake her, and that He was a friend that stuck closer than even her brother.

When she finished singing that song, it was quiet again. However, she didn't feel so lonely. She knew that He was right there with her, as He had always been. He had been with her in Japan, in London, in California, in France, in German, why would He leave her now?

"Thank you, Daddy. I am grateful for Your presence, and for this reminder that You are with me, no matter where I am. I'm so glad that when I moved, You didn't stay behind. And, I'm so glad that I didn't have to box you up and unpack you too..."

That last part made Cassie chuckle out loud, and she felt a surge of joy rush through her.

By the time she came out of the secret room, the sun had come up, and the birds were singing their morning melodies to one another. Cassie went ahead and showered, brushed her teeth, and got dressed for school. She chose to wear her favorite pair of blue jeans, a t-shirt with the word "Grace" on it in script lettering, and the white Chuck Taylors that fit her perfectly.

When the notification went off on her alarm to let her know she needed to leave to get to the bus stop, she grabbed a piece of fruit from the fridge, put her backpack on her shoulder and kissed her mom goodbye, and walked the block over to the assigned spot.

There was only one person there so far, making Cassie wonder if she was in the right place. The girl sitting on the bench didn't look happy, seemed deep in thought, and her bookbag was taking up sitting space. So, after standing there for about thirty seconds, Cassie realized that the girl still hadn't noticed her or wasn't going to move her bag, so she figured she would simply ask.

"Hi! Can I sit here?"

The girl looked up, slowly smiled, and moved the bag into her lap. "Of course," she answered shyly.

Cassie sat down and watched as other kids began arriving at the bus stop, the guys fist-bumping one another, and the girls hugging and squealing. She watched her bench mate. There was no one greeting or speaking to her. Cassie glanced down at her Chucks and then down the street as she saw the familiar yellow school bus approaching.

Looking over at the girl sitting next to her, Cassie caught her attention and said, "I'm Cassie. We just moved here. What's your name?"

The girl turned her head to look at Cassie, "I'm Trinity."

TIRED

My life had taken a downward spiral after that summer. Nothing had been the same since that time, and I feared that nothing would ever be the same again.

Unaware of how to turn it off, the scene of my nightmare continued to replay over and over again, and the results were just as devastating the last hundred times as it was the first time. Even at only 17, my life already had a definitive dividing line – that line that distinguished the former happy, carefree, and affectionate Trinity from the currently angry, distrusting, and fearful one; the pre-summer break Trinity, and the present, post-traumatic Trinity. Everyone who knew me recognized the change, and those closest to me repeatedly questioned me about the cause of this dramatic shift, but I could not bring myself to reveal the source of my trauma to any of them.

I would be the first to admit that I was broken; in fact, the truth was that I felt shattered almost beyond repair — honestly believing that if anybody could fix me, it would have to be God. So initially, I prayed over and over again, just like my parents, my pastor, and my Sunday school teachers had taught me; however, either God wasn't listening, or He simply did not care, because my pleas and petitions seemed to ring emptily in the air and yielded no evidence of hope of forthcoming help.

At this point, I didn't know what to believe anymore. I had been taught that God could do anything and that He loved everybody, which I believed with all of my heart, but now I was having a real problem trying to understand why a god who supposedly loves everybody could have allowed such a horrible thing to happen to me, and why, after I had begged and pleaded with Him over and over again, had He not taken the pain or shame away.

In my mind, I had little hope of actually being fixed because I refused to tell anyone other than God (including Cassie) what had happened. I mean, why bother dredging up painful details to tell others, if it was not going to help?

And since God was obviously not listening to me, I would simply stop talking to Him, accepting a reality that I must be the only person in the whole universe who was so bad that God could not, did not love. With that being the case, I no longer had anything to say to Him.

Meanwhile, I continued to have ongoing headaches

and stomachaches because this would grant me temporary reprieves. After all, these aches and pains were very real. My repeated complaints about them had resulted in several trips to the family doctor and other specialists. Unfortunately, not one of them could find a physical reason for these issues, suggesting that it was most likely a symptom of some emotional or hormonal imbalance sparked by either puberty or some other unknown factor.

Nevertheless, all they could offer was some medication that made me feel funky and only provided temporary relief from the discomfort, without addressing the root cause of my issue, which continued to eat away at my entire being like a rapidly spreading cancer.

I had been going to counseling for well over a year and a half by now and had already seen more than a few different counselors — and wasn't overly impressed with any of them. They were either trying too hard to be my "friend," or they saw me as just another troubled youth from the Black Bottom community on the west side of Lakeland.

The evil that had rocked my world was hundreds of miles away, tucked in the quiet, seemingly safe surroundings of a place where my mom and dad had sent me to spend summer months with family. My monster was clean-shaven and well-dressed, hiding behind a smile and loving words on the surface, but then switching into something so hideous that just the thought of its stale, liquored breath hissing vile threats and lewd comments in the dark still churns my stomach.

This monster had stolen far more than any object you could attach a dollar amount to. It had destroyed my sense of safety and security, and more importantly, a sense of self-worth that had altered my entire world for what seemed likely to be the rest of my life. In essence, this monster had issued a death sentence the moment its evil had accosted me and snuffed out the light of my young soul. So, I resolved that a mere human did not have the wherewithal to reclaim or restore what this soul-snatcher had taken; because not only did they need to have the ability to reclaim my soul, they would also be required to possess the power to resurrect it.

So, I have now decided that this morning will be my last morning to wake up! I'm so tired. Who needs homecomings, and yearbooks, and senior ditch days? I can't even think about another lunch period in the cafeteria, let alone what I'm going to do after graduation!

I'm so alone. I don't want to do this anymore.

Mom and Dad had both left for work, and my two younger brothers were already at school, and Aaron was away at college — so the house was empty. Barefoot, and still in my sleepers, I went downstairs and peered outside of the living room window, where I saw Cassie approach the bus stop and stand at our usual meeting spot. After a short while, she glanced over at the house, but I don't think she saw me. I knew that she was waiting for me, looking for me, but I just couldn't... not one more day.

Within minutes, the bus came, and after everyone had boarded the bus, Cassie being the last to get on, it pulled off. I watched until it had turned the corner before closing the curtain, making sure the doors were locked, setting the alarm to the house, and stopped by my mother's bathroom to get her bottle of Percocet that she had just refilled the day before and a glass of water. Then, I went down the hall to my bedroom and closed the door.

As I sat back on the bed, I grabbed my laptop, opened Google mail, and started a new email — addressing it to my parents, to my eldest brother Aaron, and to Cassie — to let them know how much I love and appreciated them.

When I finished hitting the send button, I shut down the laptop and turned off my cell phone. Taking the pills from my nightstand, I prepared to go back to sleep.

The knock on my front door was at first gentle, and I ignored it. But then it became incessant and persistent. I couldn't imagine who would be at our house at this hour of the morning — Mom hadn't said anything about appointments or any work being done. Plus, no one was supposed to be here anyway. Hesitantly, I put the pill bottle back on the nightstand, got out of bed, and crept back downstairs to peek out the window to see who was in the driveway.

It was Cassie!

Knowing that I would not be able to ignore her, I turned off the alarm system and opened the front door. Cassie looked at me for a few seconds, as if trying to read me. . . and then gently asked, "What's wrong?"

WAKING UP

*A*s Trinity stood looking into Cassie's puzzled face, her tears resumed their flow, cascading freely from her eyes. At that moment, there was a strange vacillation of emotions brewing within her; she didn't know whether to be angry, disappointed, or relieved that her friend had read her goodbye forever letter before she'd even had an opportunity to swallow the pills that now sat on her nightstand.

So, for the next few seconds, they just stood there in complete silence, both with their faces wet with tears. Trinity quickly realized that her plan was canceled and accepted the reality that maybe this was for the best. As odd as it seemed, she was not that keen on dying; she simply wanted the recurrent nightmare, the unrelenting fear, and the accompanying pain to cease. Peering into her bestie's eyes, she saw a level of sorrow she had only seen when looking at her own reflection in the mirror and was sure that she never wanted to be the initiator or instigator of that degree of pain for anyone; especially those she loved.

All of the defenses and walls she had so strategically constructed over the years seemed to disintegrate and crumble as she melted into Cassie's arms. She had nothing left... no fight, no plan... nothing. But then the recognition that someone was standing there holding her up in her worse moment began to occupy her thoughts. Where had the strength come from for her friend to support her so firmly while still conveying such tenderness of touch? She could not begin to understand or explain it, and in her broken state, all that mattered was her appreciation of its presence.

When Cassie did speak, she repeated the question she had asked when Trinity initially opened the door, "Trin, what's wrong?" Her voice was as sweet and soothing as it was on the day that they first met at the bus stop. There was an unexplainable energy and a light that seemed to emanate from within her when she spoke as if supernaturally charged by some unseen force.

"I...I...and she began to sob uncontrollably again. Try as she might, Trinity could not bring herself to put into words the hideous assault she had suffered that awful summer. Cassie sat patiently and gently comforted her friend. As Trinity's sobbing subsided, Cassie suggested that they go back to her house. She reminded Trinity that her house was empty because her parents were at work and her brother was still in school. Trinity nodded in agreement with Cassie's suggestion, and they both arose from the sofa.

"Can I help you get more clothes?" Cassie offered.

Trinity simply nodded, pointed towards the staircase, and whispered, "They're on my bed," and with that, Cassie disappeared up the stairs.

When Cassie returned, Trinity asked, "How did you get here so quickly? I saw you getting on the bus."

"I waited for you, but when you didn't come, I had to go or be left behind. Since I didn't have you to talk to, I decided to scroll through my phone. I saw your message when it popped in, and after I read it, I waited til all the other kids got off and pleaded with Miss Betty to bring me back home. She didn't really want to because it's against school policy, but I insisted it was an emergency, so she reluctantly agreed to drop me back off if I promised not to tell anyone. I'm glad she did because otherwise I would have had to call my mom to come get me, which meant I'd have to tell her about your letter, and she would have called your parents. . .and well, you can but imagine the scenario from there. Plus, by the time my mom could leave work, pick me up and get me here..."

Cassie's voice trailed off, and she began to cry again. "I don't even want to think about the ending to that version."

Trinity saw the spark once again leave her friend's eyes

as Cassie wept quietly. "Thank you, Cassie, I don't know what I'd do without you." With that, Trinity stood, placed the clothes in her backpack, and reached over for Cassie's hand. She then set the alarm, locked the door, and they walked to the sidewalk that led to Cassie's house.

They walked pretty much in silence for the few blocks that separated their homes, except for the occasional humming from Cassie. Cassie's singing voice was even more melodious than her speaking voice, and her singing was one of the few things that offered Trinity any measure of peace and joy. Once they reached their destination, Trinity followed Cassie into the kitchen, where Cassie was preparing to make snacks.

"Hungry?" she asked as Trinity entered the kitchen. But before Trin could respond, Cassie chuckled slightly and answered her own question, "No one can resist my culinary snack concoctions!" she dramatically exclaimed, waving the knife and spoon in the air, and causing Trinity to literally laugh out loud.

They made their way to Cassie's room, snacks in hand, and dropped their backpacks on the bed; then, without discussion, headed into Cassie's secret space. After a few bites of their snacks, Cassie looked at her friend, offered her a benevolent smile, and asked, "So, what's the goings-on, my friend?"

Trinity put down her plate, took in a deep breath, and

inched closer to Cassie. Cassie reached over and took Trinity's hands, and then patiently waited.

"Well, remember I told you about my cousin Mani and how close we used to be?" Cassie nodded, and Trinity continued. "I was spending a long weekend at her house; it was the first day, and everything was going fine..."

As Trinity continued to share the events of that weekend and, for the first time, share how those events had led to the depression and insecurities she currently suffered, Cassie sat silently weeping and uttering a silent prayer for her best friend. When Trinity finished, they were both sobbing again.

Cassie reached over and enveloped Trinity in a long hug and whispered in her ear, "I'm so sorry this happened to you, Trin...so very sorry. I know it took a lot for you to talk about it. Thank you for trusting me enough to share."

Trinity slid slowly into the fetal position and rested her head in Cassie's lap. Cassie began to sing very softly as she massaged Trinity's temples. And for the first time in a very long time, Trinity felt her soul-stirring from its slumber. She finally felt safe again, and with Cassie's voice as her lullaby, drifted off to sleep.

EPILOGUE

*I*t appeared that the vast majority of the Kingdom had accepted the King's invitation to attend this most joyous occasion. The palace was splendidly adorned and was breathtaking to behold. The combination of the sights, sounds, and smells created a truly euphoric effect; nothing was like it in all creation.

As the guests approached the front entrance, they were greeted by the beautiful music resonating throughout the massive hallways. It was as if the very walls themselves echoed every note sung by the enormous angelic choir whose voices blended in perfect harmony and every accompanying note of the orchestra whose instrument sections blended perfectly. Not only did the music fill your ears with its sound, your entire being experienced the musical rendering.

The invitation that each guest received specified the

exact section and row that was reserved for them. And, as they arrived, they were escorted to their section and seat by a Royal Hospitality Assembly Member. The seating was arranged so that each guest's seat coordinated with their graduate section. All of the graduates had arrived several hours earlier to receive final instructions and assemble for the procession. Because they were massive in number, it was nearly impossible for them to recognize anyone outside of those in their section.

As the last of the guests were ushered to their seats, the choirs rested, and the trumpets sounded — indicating the King's arrival and the beginning of the ceremony. At the sound of the last trumpet blast, each being within its sound, including those in the processional, promptly knelt in honor and reverence to the King of Kings. Then in unison, as if rehearsed for precision, each guest quietly took their seat as the members of the procession stood motionless until time to move forward.

Suddenly the procession was underway with the Archangels, Michael, Gabriel, Raphael, Uriel, and Joel, leading the way. Angels with flaming swords followed immediately behind them, as the squadrons of the King's Army followed in formation, and Seraphim flew overhead singing Holy, Holy, Holy as the King was carried in and seated upon His throne. Directly behind the Army was the great hosts of graduates and those being promoted to higher ranks within the angels' leagues. It truly was a majestic sight.

The King stood to greet all in attendance calling each and every one by name. When He spoke one name, He spoke every name, all at once, but each one heard their name clearly without any confusion. As the choir presented another musical offering, the Headmaster of the school and his designated assistants, the Archangels, and other honored participants each took their places on the stage. As each graduate's name was called and their position read, their diplomas were passed down, and the King Himself blessed it and presented it with a Royal kiss to each recipient.

Tera smiled with great joy when Sasha's name was called, and she witnessed the holy kiss bestowed upon her friend's face. She wished that she could see the expression on Sasha's face when her own name was read, and she stepped onto the stage. Because the King knew her unspoken desire, He flashed Sasha's face in Tera's spirit as she received her diploma and holy kiss; she smiled at the wonder and joy that filled Sasha's heart as she realized that Tera had also received and had completed her earthly assignment.

When all the pomp and circumstance had ended, and the King had offered the benediction for that particular gathering, Sasha — in true Sasha fashion — vacated her seat in a flash and combed the massive crowd trying to locate her friend. It took everything within her not to spread her new wings and take flight over the crowd to find her friend. Almost instinctively, she let her heart continue the search... and within no time, she had located Tera, and they stood hugging and kissing each other. Sasha began to fire what seemed like a thousand questions in succession at Tera, and Tera chuckled as she recognized her friend's spirit.

"Wait, Tera – when did you...where was your... how did you leave after me but get back the same time?"

Tera waited for the barrage of questions to cease, them she calmly attempted to answer each without dishonoring the confidentiality code they were all held to. "Just as I was about to leave after you were called in, I received my envelope and was given my assignment, and after informing my parents, I left immediately. I was assigned a high schooler who had suffered great trauma and had lost touch with..."

Before Tera could finish, Sasha said, "her soul?"

"Yes," Tera answered, looking somewhat puzzled.

"She was angry with God and had abandoned her faith?" Sasha continued.

"Wait, Sasha. How did you..."

"How did I know?" Sasha finished.

Immediately, all of the pieces began to click together. They both stood speechless and in amazement. In an instant, memories of their joint earthly assignment flooded their memory as the King stood smiling off in the distance.

They embraced again as Sasha whispered to Tera, "We were together before the earth was formed."

"And we'll be together throughout all eternity," Tera added.

Leaving the Grand Ballroom, Sasha reached out for Tera's hand, and asked, "Wanna test out these new wings?

Tera gleefully nodded her head in agreement, took hold of Sasha's hand, and together they spread their wings... and began to soar. In the rush of wind they left behind, you could hear the faint sound of giggling.

THE ADVENTURES OF CHANDLER AND THE TRAVELING PRAYER SHAWL

SHELLY SHELTON

*M*y mom always told me that prayer changes things. Actually, both of my parents talk a lot about how God has changed their lives through prayer; so, it makes sense that I find myself praying a lot!

Mom loves it when I call her to let her know that I just left church with dad. She gets so excited. I'm surprised my name isn't "Chandler Jesus Christ" instead of Chandler Shelton, as much as my parents talk about Him! Mom told me that when she was younger, she loved this TV show called *Friends*. She said there were some really cool people named Monica, Rachel, Phoebe, Ross, Joey... and Chandler. She loved the name Chandler! That's why she and Dad gave me that name.

I never know what to say when people ask, "CJ, what do your parents do?

See, Mom (or Shelly, as she is known to the rest of the world) has several jobs; she decorates, speaks to women in other countries, owns other homes, and sells houses. Dad says she's a jack of all trades. I don't quite understand what that means, though. A jack of all trades? "Slap me silly" as Grandma says, which means I have no clue what the heck that means. Lol!

My dad, Jaylen, is a doctor – a heart doctor. I think it's called a cardiologist. I just checked the spelling on that. I'm a stickler for spelling. I love to be in spelling bees. Last year, I came in second place in our state's spelling bee. I have a bunch of index cards in my room with big words on it; it keeps my mind busy when I'm focused on practicing spelling words.

Anyway... My parents are pretty cool. I just miss my mom all the time. Did I say she's also a motivational speaker? She travels around the world with other speakers talking to women's groups. I know she's on television a lot and on flyers online. Dad's always bragging about her. I think he misses her as much as I do.

Well, Chandler Jaylen Shelton is my full name, but my friends at school call me CJ "the Traveler" because I'm known as the kid with the traveling prayer shawls and I always have one with me. I guess it's a weird thing to do considering I am only eleven years old and most kids my age aren't carrying a shawl around with them... and even if they did, probably not calling it a prayer shawl.

I first started using one when I was eight. People couldn't believe the things I said and did at such a young age. Mom always said I was an "old soul." In fact, when she started telling people about what I did and writing about it, publishers didn't want to publish her book, telling her that most eight-year-olds don't talk this way.

Still, it was true. And, as you can imagine, there is a story behind it. I guess now is a great time to tell you all about it. So, where should I start?

Hmmm... well, we had just gotten out of school for the summer, and one day, I was sitting in my room looking out the window with a pair of binoculars I had made out of wire and glass and some other stuff. I use them that to check out the scenery outside.

Yeah, I'm a nerd. But I think nerds are cool now.

Our three-story house has stone on it and a nice driveway that curves around the side to the garage. My room is on the second floor facing the street. I get to see the entire row of houses on our street... *and* the street behind it.

Everyone's house is really pretty. Some of them have brick and some have stone, like ours; however, there's one house that really stands out to me. It's kind of weird looking and we rarely see anyone there. It's the only house not made of stone or brick. Instead, it has blue siding and yellow shutters. It appears to be really old... like it was here before the other houses were built. Mom says it stands out like a sore thumb.

Months before, I noticed an older lady with gray hair come out of that house. She had a cane and was walking really slow. She came out with a gentleman who had a sign in his hand. Hmm... now that I'm thinking about it – I wonder what they were up to. My binoculars weren't able to see what was written on the sign.

I begin to check out all of the leaves on the ground. It's kind of strange because June isn't usually this cool. Still, the grass is really bright and green. Dad is always outside on his lawnmower mowing it; he's a stickler for keeping the grass looking "like carpet." He's taught me how to use the weed-whacker to trim the edges, and I also plant flowers and keep the grass from growing in mom's flower bed.

Oh... I see Billy, the kid next door, riding his bike. I know he's at home by himself today because I saw his parents leave earlier. Boy, do I know what it feels like to be at home alone – or with at least one of my parents always gone – since both of my parents work a lot.

I think even what we eat can become a cool thing. Like... I love hamburgers with peanut butter and jelly. They are so good! Mom thinks it's terrible to eat that way.

Anyway, one of my best friends is Makayla. She's awesome! She lives across the street from me and we do everything together. We are both in the 6th grade and we try to take all of our classes together.

Mom says Makayla keeps me straight and reminds her of herself when she and dad met in college.

Makayla tells me that I dress "preppy." I like buttoned-up shirts with shorts, long socks, and Chuck Taylor sneakers. I have five pairs of Chuck Taylors: white, black, red, blue, and pink. Sometimes my clothes match and sometimes they don't. I think I dress differently when I go to church though. I like to wear shorts *with a tie* with my Chuck Taylors.

Ohhh... well, I guess it's not that different than my everyday gear, huh? LOL!

Girls at school love to put their hands through my hair. My hair is curly – kind of fluffy, I guess. Mom says that when she and dad first started dating, Dad used to play with his curls whenever he was stressed. I find myself doing the same. I think she gets a kick out of seeing how I do things like my father.

Hey... wait a second!

I just saw a weird guy walking down the street with a bag on his back. Hmmm... I've never seen him before. I gotta call Makayla on the traveling Walkie-Talkies I made to see if she's seen this guy before; he looks out of place. Dad says I'm the Inspector Gadget of the neighborhood. I don't know who Inspector Gadget is. He said it was some sort of cartoon he used to watch when he was a kid that had a goofy, tall guy on it. There was also a dog named Brain and a girl named Penny.

"Makayla, you there? Breaker, breaker 1-9. Makayla, are you there? I see a suspicious guy walking down the street. I've never seen him out here before."

Less than a minute later, I see a head pop up in her front room window and my receiver crackled. "Roger that, CJ! I see him. He looks weird. His clothes look

really old. Wow, he looks sad. There's a bag on his back. I'm trying to see what the bag says, but I can't from here. I think I'll go outside to get a closer look."

"Makayla, I don't think you should do that!" "Okay, if you say so. I will stay put!"

Relieved, I radioed back. "Are your mom and dad home today?"

"No, it's just me. Jenny was supposed to come over and stay with me, but she got sick at the last minute. So, they keep calling and checking on me about every thirty minutes to make sure I'm okay. I already skyped with mom and did a google- hangout with dad. What about you? Are your parents home?"

Nope. I'm home alone too. It's okay, though. How's your dog, Snowball, doing?" "He's okay. I don't know what I'd do without him. I get tired of doing homework, playing games, or looking at TV by myself. Now that we are out of school for the summer, I don't know what to do with myself. Mom still hasn't given me a cell phone yet. She thinks a cell phone will keep me from being focused on things

I need to be doing. I have been so bored today that I've already done all of my chores and cleaned my room. I've been reading and playing with Snowball. But now, he's fallen asleep on my bed. I guess he was bored, too!"

"That's funny! What are you reading?"

"I'm reading a really great book. Mom and dad have a house rule that we all must read every day. I'll tell you all about it when I'm finished."

"Okay cool, I tell you... our parents must be related or something. My parents have the same rule – *read every day*. Plus, mom gives me a word of the day. I have to write it, find the meaning of it, and call five people and use the word differently in a sentence with all of them. So, each day, I call the same five people: Grandma, Mom, Dad, Aunt Kesha, and Uncle Earl. Hey, I just remembered... I still haven't called my aunt and uncle with my word in a sentence, and they don't play when I don't call with my word in a sentence. I will check with you later, bud. I gotta run. I'm out!"

"Okay. 10-4 good buddy!" Makayla replied, just before I heard the ringtone from my tablet alerting me to a Skype call coming in.

"Hey, mom!"

"Hey, baby. What are you doing?"

"I just got off with Makayla. She's home alone today."

"You're not going out the house are you, Chan?"

No, mom! I told Makayla not to either. When are you coming home? Are you still in the Bahamas?"

"No, honey. I'm in Jamaica."

"Jamaica? Mom, I thought you said the Bahamas?"

"I'm on this tour with other speakers, honey. I talked to your dad about all of us going on vacation since you're out of school now for the summer! Would you like that?"

"Yes, mom! I would love to!" I replied, immediately excited. Then, I watched as my mom's eyes began to well up with tears. I could tell she was upset. "Mom, what's wrong?"

"I just got a call from your Aunt Kesha before I connected with you. She has cancer. Do you know what cancer is, son?"

"No mom. What's cancer?"

"Cancer is a really bad thing, honey. It is an illness, so your aunt is very sick.

She has what's called breast cancer. She wanted to talk to you about it, okay? As a matter of fact, she's still waiting for you to call her with your word sentence, so perhaps you can talk to her about this too, okay?"

"Okay, mom!"

After Mom disconnected our Skype call, I tried to google hangout my dad to let him know, but he didn't respond. So, I sent him a message.

Mom had said she wanted Aunt Kesha to tell me about cancer, but I couldn't wait that long. So, I got on my walkie-talkie and connected with Makayla. She didn't know what cancer was either. I wanted to understand more before I called my aunt, so Makayla and I jumped on YouTube.

I put "breast cancer" in the search bar and then watched video after video of people with bald heads – kids, adults, men, women. I became so sad that I began to cry.

THE BIG REVEAL

*A*unt Kesha is a close friend of my mom. But, they're so close that I've been calling her my aunt since I was a baby. She used to babysit me, and we go over to her house a lot. My dad is close to Aunt Kesha's husband, Earl. They have two boys, Dallas, and Austin – a set of twins – who are my age. My birthday is February 10th and theirs is February 12th. Mom and Aunt Kesha were in the hospital at the same time and mom had me two days before my aunt had her sons.

Aunt Kesha and Uncle Earl also have a daughter. Her name is Paris. But, Paris is 19 and in college.

Wait... is that Dad pulling up in the driveway? Yes, it is! I run downstairs to meet him.

"Dad, did you know about Aunt Kesha?" "Hmmm... what are you talking about son?" "Did you know that she has breast cancer?"

"Well, yes. But, how did you know about that? Did your mom tell you?"

"Yes, she told me when we talked earlier today."

"Your mom is not handling the news well. She and your Aunt Kesha have been friends since college. They're sorority sisters and the best of friends!"

"Dad, I looked at a lot of videos on YouTube. It was showing a lady that was really down. She was so tired. She said her name was Natalie; I kept looking at all of her videos. She kept talking, Dad, about how tired she was and taking something called chemo. Dad, she had a bald head and her hair fell out. Then she talked about how excited she was that she would be getting hormonal therapy. I haven't researched that yet. She was excited about it though because she was hoping her hair would grow back with that. Will Aunt Kesha's hair fall out, Dad?

Natalie kept talking about not wanting chemo anymore. I think it made her hair come out. She was crying about not being able to dance with her friends and have fun. Dad, I know you work with people's hearts, but can you help Natalie? Can you help Aunt Kesha, Dad?"

Finally, when I had exhausted myself of all the initial thoughts I wanted to share with my dad, I took a breath.

"Son, let's talk. Sit down. Look, I am a cardiologist. I don't know what understanding you have about cancer. So, let me explain this briefly; however, I don't want to confuse you and I don't want you to get down by this, okay? Yes, cancer is a bad thing, son. Cancer is not our friend. But, regardless of what you have heard, your aunt is going to beat this thing. Remember in the Bible where it talks about the devil comes to steal, kill, and destroy? Well, that's sort of what cancer does. It comes to kill, steal, and destroy. It is an illness that can be very painful, and sometimes you might see your aunt sick, or moody, or just not herself. If you see her in those moments, I need you to be patient with her, okay? Give her space and allow her time to feel better.

She may be tired some days. She may not be as attentive as she usually is when you're over there. Still... you just love on her, hug her, and ask if there's anything you can do to help her so that she can rest, okay?

Look, I have a pamphlet from the National Cancer Institute that helps explain it to kids, but you still may have questions. There's something called BrainPOP that I want you to look at. It has short, animated movies that will help explain this health topic. Tim and his robot Moby discuss what cancer is; I think that will help.

You know what? I just realized that as a doctor I've never had to talk to a kid about what cancer is! But, back to your question. Yes, I work with hearts. I'm not the doctor that works with cancer patients initially. However, sometimes, the medicines they take might be a little tough and cause damage to their hearts. I specialize in what's called cardio-oncology, which focuses on patients who have had – or are currently taking – some form of cancer treatment.

Say, for example, if Aunt Kesha has issues with her heart because of the effects of the cancer or the therapy used to help fight it, then I work with her and another doctor called an oncologist to help protect her heart and keep an eye on it. Does that make sense, son? Do you understand what I mean?"

"Yes, I think so dad! So, if Aunt Kesha takes that chemo stuff, then she may have to work with you to make sure it doesn't hurt her heart. Is that right dad?" "That's right, son! But, we are going to pray and think positively that Aunt Kesha will be fine."

"Dad, can I ask you another question?"

"Sure son, what it is?"

"Can she die from cancer? Can cancer make you so sick that you die?"

Quickly, my dad reached for me and said, "Come here, son!" while hugging me tightly. The strength of his hug answered my question. I knew what that answer was. Cancer can kill.

While resting in my dad's strong arms, I began to wonder what I could do to help my aunt? Mom says that when you don't know what to do, ask God. So, I asked my dad if we could pray for Aunt Kesha.

"Of course!" he replied, before taking my hand and beginning... "Heavenly Father, in the name of Jesus, we come to You, Lord with humble hearts... thankful hearts... thanking You for this day. God, one of Your children, our friend, our sister, and aunt to my son – Kesha is sick, Lord.

Father God, we are asking You to protect her from pain and sickness. In the moments when she doesn't feel well, let her know that You're there for her. Send us to help her in her times of need. Father, restore her where she needs to be restored. Build up her energy and spirit whenever she feels down. Lord, we know that You sit on the highest throne. We love You. We thank You so much for loving us. In Jesus' Name. *Amen.*"

Normally, I simply say "amen." This time, however, I wanted to pray, too. So, when my dad finished, I began. "God, I love my Aunt Kesha. Can You help her, God? I know I'm only 11 years old, God but can You tell me where I need to be or what I need to do to help her? If You want me to stay over her house to help her, or do her chores, or help her cook, or give her something that would make her feel better, please tell me. Thank You, God.

And, God if it's okay – I want to talk to You every day about my aunt until she's better. Mom always says that You will provide for our every need. I need Aunt Kesha to get better. Thanks, God. Amen!"

My dad smiled and said, "Okay, son. God heard us. Look, I talked to your mom and Aunt Kesha on the way home. Your aunt wants to have you come over tonight for dinner so that she can talk with you, Dallas, and Austin together.

"Okay, Dad," I replied, giving him a big hug before going back to my room to wash up and get ready for dinner.

* * *

About an hour later, I was in my dad's truck and on the way to Aunt Kesha's. We had barely gotten onto the porch when the door flung open and both Dallas and Austin greeted us with big smiles.

As soon as we stepped into the house, I can smell the homemade lasagna, fried chicken, green beans, and freshly baked rolls. I'm instantly reminded of how mom cooks – when she's home.

Dad and I give everyone a big hug. I then hear the door open and a familiar voice saying, "Hi Everyone!"

Wow! It's Grandma! I quickly run to hug her.

Grandma is my mom's mom, but she is also very close to my aunt. Hmmm... I wonder why my grandmother is here. Does she know about what is happening with Aunt Kesha?

Once the others in the room had gotten a chance to hug Grandma, we all sat down for dinner in the dining room. Being the elder in the house, Grandma said the grace. I love when she says the grace; she does it differently. I can't explain it. I guess it's because she's older, but she mentions scriptures when she prays.

After dinner, while Dad and Uncle Earl went into the family room to watch football and Grandma proceeded to clean up the kitchen, Aunt Kesha took me, Dallas, and Austin into the living room to talk to us. *Uh oh, I wonder if this is when she tells us?*

"Boys, I need to share something with you."

No sooner than she had gotten those words out, the doorbell rang. Who could that be? Dag, she was just getting ready to tell us.

As my grandmother went to answer the door, we quietly waited to find out who the visitor was. Suddenly, we hear Grandma screaming with joy, so we all ran to see what was going on!

It's my mom! Hugging her tightly, I asked, "Mom, what are you doing here? I was skyping with you earlier. You didn't tell me you were coming home!"

"I know son, I wanted to surprise you and your dad. I was able to get an earlier flight," she said, hugging me back. But the moment she saw my aunt, she gently let go of me and went to hug her. And, although they tried to hold back, they both started crying.

After a few minutes, Aunt Kesha broke the hug. "I

didn't know you were coming, Sis. I just sat the boys down to talk with them."

"I know. I wanted to surprise you all. It's been weeks; I miss you all so much. I can't continue to do long tours on the road like this. Do you want me to join you?"

"Yes!" Aunt Kesha replied.

So, Grandma went back into the kitchen to finish cleaning up and we returned to the living room. Once we were seated, my aunt started again. "Boys, I don't exactly know how to say this, but I want to be completely honest with you. I have something called breast cancer. It's an illness that I will be taking a medicine called chemo for; there will be days when the medicine may make me sick.

Other days, I may be tired. My hair may come out. Tomorrow, I will have my first chemo treatment. I don't know exactly how I will handle it. So, if I come home tired, I don't want you to be concerned, okay? I want you to know I will be okay. But, I will definitely need you to give me love and more and more hugs, okay?"

All three of us jumped up and hugged her!

Dallas was the first to say something. "Mom, is this cancer thing very serious? Could you die from it?"

"Yes, son. It's very serious. We are hopeful that mommy will be okay. We will continue to pray, okay?" she replied, not fully answering his question.

I know Dallas. He understood what she was *not* saying, but he didn't press her about it. She then told us to go outside and play basketball because she wanted to talk to Mom and Grandma.

Hesitating for only a moment, I closely watch my aunt before heading out. As my mother leaned over to hold her, I could see the sadness on her face. I said a silent prayer and then went outside with Austin and Dallas.

A PRAYER SHAWL FOR AUNT KESHA

*a*fter being outside for a while, I told the guys that I would be right back. I need a bathroom break. However, on my way back, I overheard grandma talking to Aunt Kesha and Mom.

"Girls, look. Years ago, I was diagnosed with lung cancer."

My mouth dropped and I almost tripped over my own two feet. Hearing me, my mom shouted, "Chan! Get outside!"

Now, I'm not normally disobedient, but I truly wanted to understand what was going on, so I crawled down behind a table to make sure that I was unseen. Thinking that I had left, my grandma continued to share how she had lung cancer twelve years previously and that she hadn't told anyone. She said that she knew God was going to protect her and she didn't want to upset anyone. Mom was upset but said she understood.

Then Grandma said, "Kesha, you will be fine, baby. We will all be here to support you to get you through this. I had chemo, but my hair didn't come out. So, there's no certainty that it will happen to you. I know that's tough for us women since we feel our hair makes us who we are or makes us feel beautiful. But, you will be okay, sweetheart!"

As they began hugging, I quietly head back outside before I am caught snooping.

Dallas, Austin, and I play basketball until we are hot and sweaty. After coming back into the house to get water and wash our hands and faces, we go into the family room to sit with Dad and Uncle Earl. My uncle wipes tears from his face when he sees us enter the room, but not before I hear my dad say, "Kesha's going to make it, bro. I got your back!"

"Were you guys talking about mommy having cancer?" Austin asked. "Yes, son." Uncle Earl replied. "So, your mother has discussed it with you? Good. I gave her space to handle it with you guys. She wanted to do it herself but I'm here if you need me or have questions. But, just because she is going through this doesn't mean that she's going to go through this alone, okay? We are all going to be there for her – me, you boys, Aunt Shelly, and Uncle Jaylen, okay? So, we'll have to pick up a little more around the house, check on her sometimes, and things like that. We may have to think about some different things out of the ordinary to do to help her too. Okay, boys?"

We silently nodded our heads in agreement.

Uncle Earl continued. "Now, Aunt Kesha knows that you may not be able to keep this to yourself. We know that you're young and may not be able to keep this quiet. But, if you can wait on talking to someone else about it until Aunt Kesha lets you know, okay?

This time, we nod and speak in unison. "Okay!" "Yes, Sir. "Of course."

As soon as I heard Uncle Earl say *we may have to think about some different things out of the ordinary to do to help her*, I immediately began to think of a creative way that I could help her.

* * *

The next day, Aunt Kesha went to the doctor to have that chemo thing that dad talked to me about. I called Dallas and Austin to see how my aunt was feeling after she got home. They told me that she was in the bed, vomiting in a trash can they had placed beside the bed, and very tired. I feel so bad for her. I've got to do something to help her.

As I sit in my room, looking out the window with my binoculars, I try to get my mind off of things. That's when I see my next-door neighbor leaving her house; she's wearing a pink and black jacket. I'm twisting my handles on the binoculars to get a better view of the saying on the back of it. Let's see... it says:

"*I am Beating Cancer's Butt*"

Wow! That's what Aunt Kesha needs to do — beat cancer's butt!

With mom being home, I am beyond excited. Today, we are going to take care of a few errands, so when she called out for me to come on, I put away my binoculars, throw on my sneakers, and head downstairs.

First, we head to a women's shelter. Mom wants to check on some of the ladies that she's been helping there. So, we go to see Tammy, Leslie, and Crystal. Mom said they seemed to be getting better; they have jobs now and are feeling more confident about themselves.

When the director of the shelter, Ms. Shana, comes over, she said, "Shelly, we are so glad you're here. We all have missed you. These ladies get down when you're not around lifting their spirits. There's something amazing about your spirit that they attach to and don't want to let go of. Unfortunately, Leslie was just diagnosed with cancer — they found a lump in her breast. She doesn't have insurance, of course, and she's so concerned about being able to afford the treatment."

Mom was crushed. It was all over her face. I could tell that she was trying to not only think about Aunt Kesha with this cancer thing, but now Ms. Leslie too. I've got to do something.

Heading out the door on our way to the next stop, there is a lady knitting a blanket-looking thing, maybe it's a quilt. I tell mom that I will meet her in the car; I'm going to speak to this lady before I head out. My mom smiled and said, "No, I want to go over to see Ms. Linda. She's new here. She comes and helps out all of the ladies, but in a different way. I love talking to her. She's incredible. Let's both go and chat with her."

Once we found Ms. Linda in the shelter, my mom shook her hand and then asked me to introduce myself. So, I did. "Hi, I'm Chandler, Shelly Shelton's son.

"Good morning, Master Chandler. We hear a lot about you here. Your mother is always talking about how proud she is of you."

My eyes open as big as the sun. I didn't realize my mom talks about me like that. "She does?" I ask.

"Yes, of course, she does."

Mom lovingly rubbed her fingers through the curls in my hair. "Honey, I brag about you everywhere I go. You and your dad are my everything!" she said, before leaning down and kissing my forehead. Then, turning her attention back to Ms. Linda, she asked, "How are you doing today, Ms. Linda.?"

"I'm doing great Ms. Shelly! I've been crocheting my prayer shawls."

Prayer shawls? I thought to myself. Hmmm... "What are prayer shawls," I asked out loud.

"Well, there's so much pain in the world, whether it's physical, financial, emotional, or spiritual. So, years ago, I began crocheting to get through the emotional pain of going through a divorce. My husband meant the world to me and when he left, I felt alone and worthless. I would make them in different colors and pray over every stitch. Soon, I had one in every room of my house, and before I knew it, my pain had subsided, and forgiveness had moved into my heart. It did wonders!"

Mom said, "Ms. Linda, I believe in the power of prayer and miracles. I think God is using you to heal those who are going through difficult times through your prayer and warm spirit. Would you be willing to sell them? I would like to buy ten of them from you."

"Ms. Shelly, I must say this to you. Every time you come around here you spread love. You are a magnet with these ladies. They cannot wait to hear that you're coming; just your name is a blessing. In fact, I looked up the meaning of your name Shelly. It said that people with this name have a deep inner desire for travel and adventure and want to set their own pace in life without being governed by tradition. People with this name tend to be passionate, compassionate, intuitive, romantic, and to have magnetic personalities. They are usually humanitarian, broadminded and generous, and tend to follow professions where they can serve humanity. Because of who you are, Ms. Shelly, I will do one for free — just for you. In fact, I will bless you with this hot pink-colored one I'm doing right now. The remaining nine... how's $10 each sound?"

Mom was smiling from ear to ear and crying. Mom cries for almost anything I see. But, heck... even I was crying. Mom thanked Ms. Linda, opening her purse to get the cash to pay a deposit. As she wiped her tears, she exclaimed, "You know what, Linda? Two things. One, I never carry cash with me, but today I have some. And two, what color is my wallet?

"Hot pink," Ms. Linda replied.

"You could not have known that hot pink is my favorite color!"

As they both laughed, in awe of how God works in even the small details, mom gave her half of the cost of the order and said she'd give her the other when she returned to pick up the shawls later in the week.

On the way home, I asked mom what she was going to do with her new shawl. She didn't know. After a few minutes of quiet thought, I told her I'd like to actually buy it from her with my allowance and give it to Aunt Kesha. I get $5 a week for doing my chores, helping to keep the community clean, helping dad with the yard, helping mom at women's shelters or women's groups, washing my parents' cars, keeping my room clean, and maintaining my grades in school. Yes, mom and dad keep me busy!

"You don't have to do that, honey!"

"No, mom. I will pay you for this one. You can pay for the others. I know it's your favorite color, though. I can ask Ms. Linda if she will do another hot pink one for you, mom. Dad and Uncle Earl said Aunt Kesha may have difficult days and Ms. Linda said it helped with her difficult days. So, I want to give it to her and pray that God uses it to help her with difficult days from chemo. Would you be okay with that?"

Smiling, she agreed. I think she was proud of me because she got teary-eyed again.

Later that morning, after we got home from running all of the errands on my mother's to-do list, I immediately went upstairs to look for a nice gift bag and tissue paper to wrap the prayer shawl. Mom has a room that she uses for her interior decorating, so I went in there and found a really pretty white bag, cards, tissue paper, and all. I have helped mom over a thousand times wrap items for people, so I knew how to wrap the gift and bag it nicely for my aunt. When finished, I took it downstairs.

"Hey, mom and dad. Can either one of you take me over to Aunt Kesha's tonight or tomorrow?"

"What do you have there, son?" my dad asked.

I explained everything about our morning with Ms. Linda, and how she prays over every stitch. Dad was blown away. I also told him that I had bought this one from mom. "Oh, and here, mom. Here's my $10!" I said, handing her ten neatly folded singles.

She gently took the cash from my hand and put the bills into an iced tea maker she has where she stashes cash to use during the week. It also happens to be the same container where she keeps the funds used to give me my allowance.

Dad says he'll take me over Aunt Kesha's tonight. He calls Uncle Earl to be sure it's okay, and when Dad asks how she's doing, my uncle told him, "She's in the bed. Just another day of sickness. But I've cooked dinner for us, so come on over."

"We won't stay long, Earl. CJ has something for her. We'll just stop by and give him an opportunity to drop it off."

On the drive over, I asked Dad if it was okay if I prayed before we got there. "Sure, son!"

I began to pray. "God, I pray that this prayer shawl does what Ms. Linda says that it does — heal from all pain. Aunt Kesha's in pain. I want her to take this shawl with her to her doctor's appointments when she gets chemo. I want her to put it on her in her bed when she's sick at home. I want her to take it with her whenever she feels any type of pain. Heal her God. Mom says Your Word says You are a provider and a healer. If my parents trust and believe in you like that God, then so do I. Please God... heal my aunt. In Jesus' name. Amen."

"Amen... and amen!" my dad said, in agreement.

Sure enough, Aunt Kesha is in the bed. Uncle Earl told me that it was okay for me to go upstairs to see her. As soon as I enter their bedroom, she sat up and asked for a hug. I jump in the bed with her on Uncle Earl's side of the bed. Wow, she looked sick.

"How are you feeling?" I asked, already knowing the answer.

She said, "Great!" But, I knew she wasn't. I handed her the gift I had brought for her and watched with anticipation as she opened the bag and pulled out the hot pink prayer shawl.

Laughing and smiling, she said, "Wow, lil' nephew! What's this? It's beautiful... and the color is gorgeous!"

"Aunt Kesha, it's a prayer shawl. Ms. Linda crocheted it. She prays over every stitch. And, she said it's to help heal everyone from emotional, mental, physical, and spiritual pain. I bought it from mommy so I could bless you with it. I prayed with God that it would heal you and make you feel better when you're sick, Aunt Kesha! I want you to take it with you to your doctor's appointment or, whenever you're not feeling well! Okay?"

She began to cry. "Chandler, my darling, I love you so much. You know that? Thank you for blessing me with this! I will keep it with me and take it everywhere I go, nephew! It will be like a *traveling* prayer shawl, huh?"

"Yes, exactly! A traveling prayer shawl!"

We hugged and chatted for a few minutes more, and then I left the room so that my aunt could get some rest.

*L*ater that week, mom and I went back to the shelter to meet Ms. Linda to pick up the remaining prayer shawls. On the way over, we called Aunt Kesha from the car to see how she was doing.

"Chandler, honey... this prayer shawl is doing wonders," she said, excitedly! "I haven't been sick at all since you gave it to me. I take it with me in the car and place it on my legs when I drive. I place it on me at the doctor's appointments while getting the chemo. And, I'm not sick after the chemo treatments anymore; I haven't vomited in days or been tired. I love it! I love it!"

Instantly, I knew that I was on to something. If the prayer shawl could help to heal my aunt, how many more women could it help?

"Mom?" I said after she had disconnected the call. "If the shawl helped Aunt Kesha, I'm sure they can help other women. Mommy, I know you bought the other nine from Ms. Linda, but I have more money in my allowance. I would like to buy them from you, too."

There she goes — mom was crying again. She assured me that they were tears of joy; she was just moved with how proud she was of me.

I asked her if she could think of other women who were sick and could use them. She did.

We picked up the rest of the prayer shawls and then came back home. I immediately gave her $90 from my allowance before going into her interior decorating room and bagging them up like I had done with my aunt's. Each one of them was unique and pretty.

Afterward, Mom and I went to visit with each one of the ladies she knew had cancer — including Ms. Leslie from the shelter. I shared with them the story behind the shawls, how I believed in the power of prayer, and what Aunt Kesha had done with the prayer shawl.

Several weeks later, Mom showed me her social media pages. And, guess what? Each one of them had posted pictures of themselves with the prayer shawl. They were doing exactly what my aunt had done — driving with it, at the beach with it, at doctor's appointments, everywhere! They were feeling better and better every day. Their posts were going viral, and soon, other women were sending messages to my mom asking how they could connect with me and get more!

So, Mom created a social media account for me on Facebook, Instagram, and Snapchat. Within a short timeframe, not only were women tagging me and asking for prayer shawls but also some people mom called "influencers" were sharing posts about the prayer shawls!

I asked my mom, "What do we do now?"

She said, "Honey, we gotta give them what they want. Let's go and talk to Ms. Linda."

You can imagine how overwhelmed with emotion she was when we told her what was happening! She said, "I have been doing them for years. I have a large inventory of them... in a myriad of colors."

"You do?!" we both said, with surprise.

"Yes. I did those last nine just for you... with special prayers for you two and your Aunt Kesha!" Ms. Linda said.

Mom and dad worked out an arrangement with Ms. Linda and bought out her entire inventory of prayer shawls. I told them I didn't have that much money in my allowance. Mom just smiled and told me that what I was doing was blessing the world and that Ms. Linda was a Godsend. It was their joy to support us both.

Not long after this, Dad came home early from work. "Honey, why are you home so early?" Mom asked.

"I can't get anything done at work. Everyone is talking

about Chandler at the hospital. They all want a prayer shawl," he answered, pulling a large amount of money out of his pocket and placing it on the kitchen table. "This is at least $1000 from people who have given me orders to bring to you. However, not just people with cancer — but other ailments like multiple sclerosis, arthritis, ALS, high blood pressure... they all want one. They want to be relieved of the pain – even if it's for only a day.

At that moment, my parents and I decided on a plan to bless the world. They began talking to me about starting a business. Mom got us a business license, had her business partners design a website, bought trademarks, copyrights, and other stuff I've never heard of.

Now, we needed to talk to Ms. Linda again. Because, once we ran out of the initial amount that she had already sold us, we would have to figure out how to get more.

Again, Ms. Linda blows our minds. She told us that she had forgotten that there were some in a storage unit that her daughters had been adding to for years. They loved crocheting them so much that they couldn't give them away fast enough... and just stored and stored them. So, in the end, we actually had more shawls than we expected!

My parents bought every single one of them, and before long, our website went live, and the orders flooded in. We were praying over them and sending them out as quickly as they were requesting them. Even Makayla came over each day to help with packing and delivery, and the mail lady and FedEx trucks were a regular sight at our house!

By the time summer was over and school started back up, we had sold over half our traveling prayer shawls, and the hashtags #chandlertravelingprayershawl and #chandlerfightscancer became widely trended.

Can I tell you something? A much greater blessing than the volume being shipped was the amazing number of testimonies that were being shared. From all over the world, we received emails, DM's, and tags of how the prayer shawl had helped to bring comfort and healing.

My goodness, we got letters from people with breast cancer, lung cancer, prostate cancer... from Jamaica, Hawaii, London, the Philippines, St. Martin, and Paris! Many of them were written in other languages, so mom and dad would have to find someone to translate it to English to help me understand what they were sharing with me. Like, this letter for example; it was originally written in Spanish by two girls my age from Brazil, but here is the translated version:

Dear Chandler,

My sister Torie and I wanted to let you know how your traveling prayer shawls have helped our mommy and daddy. Both of our parents have cancer. Mommy has breast cancer and daddy has prostate cancer. When we heard about your prayer shawls, we bought both of them one. It has been a true miracle. At their last chemo treatment, the doctor said that neither of them had to do chemo again. The cancer was gone. We want to say thank you! Thank you, for blessing our parents with your prayer shawls. God bless you, and we hope we can meet you one day and give you a hug!

Love,
Storie & Torie

We decided to donate a portion of what we made to cancer research, and mom and dad made sure Ms. Linda and her daughters were paid well to continue making the prayer shawls. However, Ms. Linda said the money meant nothing to her; it was the vision God had given her to bless the world that was most important.

I agree. And now, three years later, I still feel the same way.

EPILOGUE

ell, that's my story. I told you it was a long one. And you know what? With all of the praying, and shipping, and social media posting, I have been a pretty busy kid. So busy that I almost forgot that I am going to turn twelve years old tomorrow. Normally, I give my parents a list of the things I want, but it has been great to help people. It's like I get a gift each time someone posts a picture of themselves with the prayer shawl and shares what our prayers have done for them.

And to think that all of this started from our faith in God to heal Aunt Kesha.

Everything has made me realize how much I love my parents and my friends. Wow... I really want to talk to my buddy Makayla. So, grabbing my walkie- talkie out of the door, I ping her. "Makayla... you there?"

No answer. Then, a chat message comes in on my tablet. "Hey, CJ. I'm out with the fam. What's up?"

I smile and message her right back:

I like you. Would you like to be my girlfriend?

Wondering what she said?

...that's a story for next time.

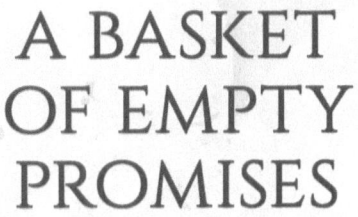

A BASKET
OF EMPTY
PROMISES

ANGEL
MILLER

CHAPTER 1

The wedding was exquisite. *I can't believe I just married this man*, Karmen thought. "All of the promises finally came through," she whispered. Mentally processing everything, she reminisced on how their love began.

Karmen and Rick dated for two years prior to him proposing. He was absolutely the man that her heart raced for. It was during the courtship that he presented her with the lovely basket her flower girl was carrying. Rick had the basket custom made, just for Karmen because he knew that she adored unique keepsakes. It was wrapped in purple, lavender, Carolina blue and ivory ribbon — some of her favorite colors.

Every birthday, holiday, special occasion, and "just because," he gave her a handwritten promise on parchment paper, and she would place it in the basket. The most recent promise was written the night before the wedding, but it hadn't been placed in the basket yet.

Instead of flower petals for the wedding, the basket was filled with every promise he'd ever made to her. Rick read several of them during the ceremony as part of his public vow and commitment to her and their union, including the most recent one, *I will always be here for you. I will always love you. I promise to never intentionally hurt you. I will never leave you nor forsake you. I will support you.*

Some of the promises were so close to God's promises for her that she knew without a doubt Rick was the one for her. She was ready to build an extraordinary life with this man. To build the life she had always imagined and dreamt of.

This was it...

Several years later...

Karmen opened the first card. It read, *Honey I love you and a love like ours is forever.* Her heart sank deep into her chest, at least it felt like it did. She opened the next card. It was worse. She couldn't believe what she read, *To the man I love...*

Every emotion imaginable flushed through the teardrops falling from her eyes. Seven years —all of the time and investments, financially, spiritually, mentally—

she had completely given her heart and soul to this man only to find out that he had been having multiple affairs with women in other cities and states. How? Why? How did he find the time? With his mother in and out of the hospital and the job, the businesses, ministry? How did he find the time to have multiple relationships? Devastated and broken, Karmen tried to gather her thoughts.

He was at work and she had to get herself together and come up with a plan to get out of this fiasco of a marriage she now wondered how she got herself into. She began to think back on all the things he said and did that didn't coincide, how his behaviors changed periodically, week to week. How he would disappear for days at a time and state that he was just taking some time to be with the fellas. She just thought he was tired. Then she remembered there were holidays and birthdays he would be away, stating he had an impromptu business trip or some other engagement in which she could not attend with him. He didn't want to be with her. What man doesn't want to be with his woman on his birthday?

The flood of memories filled her mind and she gasped. How long had this been going on? She remembered how he instigated a major argument with her for his 50th birthday and made her feel like she was smothering him and consuming his time. Where was the man she met years ago? The man who said he loved her and wanted her to have his children? Where was the man who said he wanted to make life better for her and him? She reminisced on all of their "great" memories. The flowers, gifts, hugs, and passionate kisses he showered her with whenever he was in her presence. Where was this man? It was as if this was an imposter. He had grown cold and mean spirited, lashing out at her whenever things didn't go his way.

Things were beginning to make sense and the beautifully woven fabric of their marriage was unraveling right before her eyes. Her thoughts raced and rage was taking over, "he isn't keeping all of the promises he made to me!" She screamed in emotional agony at the thought of him sharing himself with all these different women.

"How could he do this to her?" she thought. She was there from the beginning, before the money. *"This bastard!"* she screamed. Words she hadn't used in years tormented her thoughts.

Before the cars, the houses, the fame, and fortune, she helped him build his radio platform, his ministry, his businesses, the non-profit, and helped him market all of his publications. She worked behind the scenes to make sure he always looked good in the public eye. She stayed up late hours researching for connections and organizations that would benefit his endeavors. She helped take care of his elderly and sick mother and her home.

And this is how he repaid her? With this level of disrespect? How dare he? Her emotions took over again. Tears flooded her face once more. Anger and sadness combined to create an emotional tsunami that she knew only Holy Spirit could control. What was she going to do? She didn't have the strength at that moment to make any real decisions, but she knew for the night, or at least a few days, she had to get away.

Quickly, she packed some things and left him a note:

> *Going away for a few days to Savannah.*
> *I will text you when I get there.*

She didn't lack money. In addition to the resources he provided for their home, she had her own. She was well educated, owned several businesses, and worked as a tenured professor at Clarke Atlanta. She had purchased several properties, including two beautiful homes in the Bahamas and one in Grenada, before they married. The closest respite was her immaculate beach home at Tybee Island in Savannah, Georgia so she decided to travel there for a few days to regroup.

She left the cards on the table next to her note and gathered her things to put in the car. Then she pulled out her phone and checked these women's Facebook accounts to see if she could find anything that would remotely help her understand this whirlwind of information she had just discovered.

What she found nearly made her faint.

One of the women was pregnant. And he had the nerve to be engaged to her? How did they meet? Where did she come from? Texas? What in the hell was he thinking? Then she whispered, "forgive my language, God." She knew that God was on her side, but she felt abandoned and lonely right now. She couldn't tell her family or her daughter. She had a child from a previous marriage. Her family adored Rick. She couldn't tell them what was going on. The only person she could talk to was her best friend. She couldn't even call her pastor because they attended the same worship & fellowship center.

"Uggghhh, I can't stand him right now!" This *son of a* — her thoughts stopped dead. She remembered that her parents taught her to never use that type of language.

Karmen mustered up a scream like never before. She felt it come from deep inside her soul.

She had plenty of time to think on this drive. Savannah would be good for her right now. The ocean air and sun would boost her mood. She started thinking again. Was he doing this because she had gotten ill over the last two years? Karmen had been diagnosed with several chronic and energy depriving conditions causing her to suffer severe setbacks over the last year. She had been out of work for six months, however, that hadn't affected their financial position. Rick owned several rental properties in Atlanta, Charleston, and some in North Carolina as well, so they were perfectly okay with money. So, what was his reason?

She called her best friend so she could process everything. Briana answered the phone and said, "what's going on, chica?" as she always does. This time Karmen wasn't laughing, she was crying uncontrollably. She could barely speak through the tears, her asthma beginning to exacerbate. Briana responded, "talk to me, girl. What is it?"

Karmen managed to whisper through sobs, "Rick has been cheating on me. He's engaged to one of the women."

"Wait a minute, one of the women? What do you mean? There's more than one?"

"Yes, girl. He's been having multiple affairs. Apparently, the one he is engaged to is pregnant."

"What? How?"

"The two of you are always together. He's constantly busy with work or ministry, his mom. I will kill him! I can't believe he would do something like this to my friend. He's an ordained minister, a pastor. What is he thinking Karmen?

"This is bad, this is really bad. Where are you right now?"

Still sobbing Karmen said under her breath, "headed to the beach house in Savannah."

"Do you need me to come there?"

"Sure, if you can. I don't need to be by myself, I guess. I don't know what to do. I just found out I am three months pregnant also. How could he do this to me? I just don't understand.

"Bri, it will take me a few hours to drive there but take your key just in case you get there before I do. Thank you, girl, for being here. I am so devastated. I will see you soon."

"You're welcome, chica. God has a plan. Hold your head up and don't give up right now. I know this is difficult, but you will get through it.

"Rick has a lot of explaining to do but don't worry about that right now. You have to think of you and the baby now."

She turned on her Pandora app in the car and let the sounds of worship music play as she journeyed to distance herself from this pain. Flooding her car was Tasha Cobb's "For Your Glory." She needed to hear from Holy Spirit now more than ever because she was at the end of her rope.

The drive didn't take as long as she thought, or maybe she was so engrossed in her thoughts that she hadn't noticed she was driving 85 mph. Thankfully, there were no cops. She let out a huge sigh as she pulled into the driveway, *Help me Holy Ghost. I can't do this without you.*

CHAPTER 2

*K*armen turned the key in the door and stepped inside her lovely beach home. She hadn't been here in months. Briana hadn't arrived so she just sat her bags down in the foyer and perched herself on one of the bar stools separating the main living space from the kitchen. She needed to think, pray, and plan.

She looked at the exhaustive wine bar in her kitchen and thought, m*aybe I should just drink.* However, she was too overwhelmed with despair to really do anything. Of course, she knew she couldn't drink her favorite Moscato right now. The baby was more important, but the thought was tempting. A hot bath and relaxing music would do the trick. She made her way upstairs to run the water and attempt to relax from the day's disappointments.

Rick would occasionally come with her, yet he hadn't been lately. This was her safe place. This was the first property she purchased after graduating from college and she loved the spacious rooms. She worked with a major designer in the area and developed many of the plans herself, but the details of the elaborate home didn't even matter right now. Although, this was where Holy Spirit spoke to her and said she would someday minister to women around the world, she was broken and needed restoration herself. Her entire world shattered, she couldn't think about anything else. This is where she and her sister-friends came for retreats and where she would host some of her women's gatherings. She loved it here. Financially, she knew she would be okay if she and Rick got a divorce. However, the thought of raising this baby alone bothered her.

She managed to make her way upstairs to the master bedroom after exhaling and turned on the shower in her spa-designed master bath and let the bathroom steam up. She wanted to relax, not wanting anything to stress her anymore. Briana was right. She had to think of herself and her unborn baby. Rick didn't know yet. She hadn't told him because she was waiting for just the right time, but then she found those cards.

Every unthinkable word she could muster came to mind as she thought about what he had been doing. *Damn him*, she thought, *I just can't believe he would do this to me. All those promises! Wait! Where is my basket anyway?*

Overwhelmed with emotion, she began searching

every room in the house. She knew it was here somewhere, she just needed to find it. All she wanted to do was read them one more time then burn them and throw the ashes in the ocean.

Finally, she found it. She began reading them one by one. She decided that she and Briana would sit out on the beach and have a waiting to exhale moment. Filled with a range of emotions, she fell to her knees and began crying out to God, "he made me promises, Lord. He stood before you, our family and friends, lying about these promises! Why did you let this happen?"

Immediately she repented. In her heart, she knew that cursing him was not the solution. Yet she didn't know how to pray for him or herself. She only managed to say, "Father help me. I need you now."

She climbed up on the bed after pulling out one of her favorite biographies by Maya Angelou, "All God's Children Need Traveling Shoes." Maya's prolific words always had a way of uplifting her spirit. Although she had read the book dozens of times already, she felt she needed a powerful distraction and began reading Chapter 1:

The breezes of the West African night were
intimate and shy, licking the hair, sweeping through
cotton dresses with unseemly intimacy, then
disappearing into the utter blackness. Daylight was
equally insistent, but bolder and more thoughtless.

*It dazzled, muddling the sight. It forced through my
closed eyelids, bringing me up and out of a
borrowed bed and into brand new streets.*[1]

She checked her phone. Rick hadn't called. She
assumed he either wasn't home yet, or he was trying to
figure out a way to explain his foolish behavior. Briana sent
a text saying that she would be there early in the morning.
Karmen responded, "okay, see you soon & drive safely.
Goodness and mercy follow you."

The lateness of the hour was at hand and Karmen soon
drifted off to sleep. She was awakened by the sound of her
phone ringing. Startled, she looked at the screen.

It was Rick.

She just let it ring. She didn't feel like talking to him.
Checking the voicemail, a few more choice words entered
her mind. She knew she couldn't speak with him while she
was angry. But maybe he needed to hear the anguish in her
voice. Maybe he needed to hear her crying or feeling the
pain of his betrayal. She checked the clock, it was 5:00 am.

Why was he just calling her? Of course, he was out
with one of his side chicks. She put the phone on the
nightstand and just began to cry out to God, "Father, I
know I am not perfect. I know that I have made many
mistakes. I just don't understand why Rick would do such
things to destroy our family and home. I have been faithful
and loyal, committed to him. I am not an unattractive

woman. I am educated and have offered him everything he could have ever needed or wanted in a wife. Why? Why me?"

At that moment, she heard the sound of keys at the door. Briana ran up the stairs to greet her friend. They had not seen each other since Karmen had been out of work a few months prior. Not to mention, Briana had been traveling back and forth to Wilmington, North Carolina to see family and she just launched her coaching business earlier this year. The last girl's retreat was at Karmen's beach home in the Bahamas. All of them had declared that they would do something new with their lives each year and they would add something inspiring to their gratitude box daily.

Not only did Karmen have a gratitude box, she had a basket of promises that Rick had given her early in their courtship. She would periodically read each promise as a reminder of their "perfect love," which wasn't so perfect anymore. Tears began rolling down her pecan tan face. She was a beautiful woman, 100% of everything he needed as a wife. She believed she had the most wonderful life until now. Briana grabbed a tissue box from the table across the room. She knew her friend needed her more than ever now, so she just sat there and rocked Karmen to sleep, wiping her tear-stained face, as she sang "That's What Friends Are For."

CHAPTER 3

She woke up thinking about that basket of promises Rick had given her. None of them meant anything anymore. Nothing he said or did mattered anymore. It was all a lie. The phone rang again. It was Rick calling for the third time. He left multiple messages and texts. Karmen ignored his calls and texts while looking out the panoramic, picturesque windows in her bedroom. The curtains were on a timer and opened like clockwork every morning at sunrise, 6:15 am. She could see the ocean waves splashing upon the beach, even from the bed. The balcony overlooking the beach was a custom feature she requested when the home was built. The sounds of seagulls echoed in the distance.

Her sense of smell had worked great since she became pregnant, Briana was cooking breakfast as usual. Briana and her sister Shalene always cooked breakfast. Karmen inwardly laughed as she remembered all of their crazy girl's nights consuming delicious food, dessert, and wine — laughing and sitting on Shalene's patio, roasting marshmallows over the fire pit.

Thoughts racing, her attention drifted back to the basket of promises. Where was it? She always left it at the beach house because whenever she was here, she would sit on the beach at sunset, reading each one. Perusing the tiny messages of love made her feel closer to Rick when they were apart.

> *I will always love you, baby. I will never intentionally hurt you. I will be here when you wake up in the mornings and when you go to bed at night. I promise to love you, cherish you and protect you. I promise to support you...*

The list continued. What did those words mean now? Absolutely nothing.

Karmen pulled herself out of bed and went to the bathroom to freshen up. Staring in the mirror she just wondered how her life came to this point of failure. She went downstairs to check on Briana and demolish this great smelling food. Her best friend had outdone herself. She made toast, turkey sausage links, bacon, grits, scrambled eggs, hash browns, bagels with cream cheese, mimosas, and served fresh fruit. "What a spread, chica! Where did you get all of this?"

Briana laughed and said, "I wanted to make sure you and my niece or nephew are well taken care of while I am here. I stopped at the grocery store on my way in."

Since she began working for herself, Briana had the freedom to make her own schedule. She committed to staying at the beach with Karmen for several days if necessary. She could still do some remote online coaching for many of her clients.

The phone rang again. Karmen said, "It's Rick, Briana. He's been calling for the last few hours and has sent several messages. I don't want to talk to him right now. He knows that I know about the women."

Briana responded, "I don't blame you, but you will have to speak to him eventually. And you have to tell him about the baby."

"I know but if I speak to him now, I feel as if I will unleash quite a bit of anger toward him."

Briana replied, "That's understandable. Look what he's done. He's destroyed your family, home, and everything you both have worked so hard to attain. What if his partners find out about this? Or even the media, the church? What then? He can't possibly think this is acceptable."

Shaking her head, Briana continued, "Or maybe he does. Have you considered your next move, chica?"

Karmen looked Briana in the eyes and tears began to fall.

"No. I don't want to raise this child alone. But he's leaving me no choice. He clearly doesn't want to be with me, and I don't understand why. What is wrong with me?"

"Stop it, Karmen," Briana interrupted. "I am not going to let you do this to yourself. You are not the problem. He is. You have done everything you can to be a good wife to him. There were numerous times men approached you and wanted you to be with them, but you turned every one of them down. Each time. There is something wrong with him, not you. You chose him out of anyone you could have had in your life and you loved him completely as God wanted you to. This is NOT your fault. Do you understand what I am saying? This is not your fault girl."

Steaming mad, Briana slammed her cup down on the table. "I am so angry with him right now! How dare he do this to my friend!"

Karmen's phone rang again. It was Rick calling. Sobbing, she decided to answer. "What do you want, Rick?"

He sounded desperate but she didn't care. "Baby, please listen. I didn't mean for things to happen like this."

"Then how did you plan for them to happen, Rick? This woman in Texas—she's pregnant with your baby?" Well guess what, so am I! How could you do this to me, to us, to our unborn baby? You have destroyed our family and for what? What do these women have that I don't have?"

"I am sorry Karmen, I am so sorry. Please come home so we can talk this out."

She wouldn't let him answer, "what the hell is there to discuss? Clearly, you made your choices. What do we have to talk about? Multiple women Rick. Look what you have exposed me to. And why? Please tell me why?"

She paused to see how he would respond.

"Baby I don't know. I was unhappy with you being gone all the time for your businesses and ministry."

"What? Are you serious? You are gone just as much and look how much time we actually do spend together. That's a cop-out and a weak excuse for what you have done. So now what is there to discuss? Alimony, child support—ummm that's all I think we have to talk about right now. Bye, Rick. I am done with this and you! The next time you hear from me will be concerning divorce papers."

She couldn't believe what she had just heard. "He destroyed our marriage over me being gone helping build our businesses and lifestyle? Is he serious? No there has to be more to this!"

Thinking out loud, Karmen blurted, "that selfish jackass! —let me stop. I am sorry, God. I don't mean to call him ugly names. But I am so angry with him right now!"

"Karmen, you have to calm down. For the sake of the

baby. Think strategies at this juncture. You see what you are dealing with. Clearly, he has lost his mind and his behavior is beyond unacceptable. Now we have to be smart about how you move forward."

Karmen grabbed a tissue, wiped her tears, and said, "you are absolutely correct sister friend. I will have my attorney contact his attorney on Monday morning. Meanwhile, I am going to enjoy the rest of my few days here and get this off my mind. Let's hit the streets, Briana."

CHAPTER 4

*B*riana hadn't been out in forever. She realized she needed this time just as much as Karmen did. Savannah's River Street had always been lit, daytime or evenings, with tourists and locals. There was a lot to do there and just being near the water was refreshing. Briana and Karmen decided to stop at the Saltwater Taffy factory and a few shops before dancing, and then finally to one of Karmen's favorite restaurants along River Street, *Vic's On the Strip.*

Immediately Karmen's mind shifted to a blast from the past, during her college days when she would visit here. There was only one man who had captured her heart more than Rick. He brought her here often. He was fine — Justin. She hadn't been reminded of him until now. The smell of his cologne seemed to fill her nostrils and she daydreamed about how gorgeous this man was then, and how he treated her so well. She received her favorite flowers almost weekly — tulips, lilies, mixed bright carnations, and sometimes he would send a bouquet of pink, yellow, and red roses. Justin stood 6'2" tall, athletic build, chocolate as chocolate could be with a beautiful bright smile that would light up any room and his voice, oh my gosh, it was mesmerizing— "hello Karmen," a familiar voice startled her and she turned around.

She gasped and so did Briana. She was in shock for a moment. He touched her arm. She couldn't believe her eyes. Here was this man, the one she had just been daydreaming about. Justin was right there in front of her. Struggling to form her words, "ummm—uuhhh, Justin? Ummm—wha—what are you doing here?"

He chuckled, "you look as if you are surprised to see me. I come here often, as we used to do. It is still my favorite place."

Karmen, still in disbelief, managed to gather herself quickly—while Briana stood by, just as shocked, "Karmen, I am going to the ladies' room. I will be right back while you guys catch up."

"Yes, I am surprised to see you. I apologize, I was flabbergasted for a moment." She didn't have the guts to tell him that at that moment her every thought was about him.

"Briana and I were here for a few days to unwind.

What are you doing here? Oh, never mind. You just told me that you come here often." Feeling foolish, she laughed.

"My, my, my. How I have missed hearing your beautiful laugh, Karmen. And you are still as beautiful as I remember. What has been going on in your life since we parted?"

Deep in her thoughts, Karmen was still amazed that this man whom she had not seen in years was standing before her and he was just as handsome, if not more than he was then. Seasoned. His salt-and-pepper gray go-tee was trimmed nicely complementing every other feature. He wore a deep purple dress shirt that snuggly caressed his upper frame. Karmen glanced at him as he spoke, her eyes soaking in every bit of his 6' stature.

She wondered, *why had we broken up? How could I have let this man go? —Oh, yes—he moved to Paris right after college.* Justin had received a lucrative offer with a company in Paris, France as the operations manager. There was no way Karmen could go to France at the time. She'd been through an ordeal with her family and was needed here in the States. They remained friends and kept in contact until Karmen got married.

He glanced at her hand. She was still wearing the stunning diamonds Rick had given her, "I see you are still married."

"Yes, I am. But what about you, Justin? Where is your wife?"

"She and I got divorced five years ago. I have been single since. I haven't found anyone else that I want to share my heart and life with. If I ever marry again, I want it to be for love. Not a situation-ship."

"I see and totally agree Justin. Marriage should be forever. So, what happened?"

"I met her not long after moving to Paris, at a business party for one of the company's partners. She was attractive but I didn't realize she was only there to meet men. We started seeing each other but we weren't in love. It was lust and we hooked up several times, just a physical thing. Then she got pregnant. I didn't want the baby to grow up without a father, so I stuck it out.

"Although I was miserable, she seemed happy just to have my son and collect a check each month. Not long after Isaiah was born, I filed for a divorce and brought him back to the States with me. Thankfully, she didn't fight me, she knew that he would have a better life with me. So here I am, single with a 10-year-old son, enjoying life."

Karmen didn't let him know that this was a welcome distraction to take her mind off her unfaithful husband. She wasn't going to disclose what was going on. *Or maybe she should.*

Deep down she was fighting the tears. This was the man she gave up for Rick. She knew back then that Justin genuinely loved her and wanted a life with her, but she could not leave the country with him.

About that time, Briana came from the bathroom. They all sat down together and conversed over dinner. Afterward, Justin asked if he could spend a little more time with Karmen, so they drove Briana back to the house and drove to the beach. The moonlight danced over the water and the conversation was enlightening. Now Karmen remembered why she loved him so, he knew just how to captivate her with his words, and he was sincere. Before driving back to get her car, Justin confessed that he still loved her and wished things could have worked back then.

"I will always love you, Karmen. You are the only woman who loved me when I had nothing."

"Justin, my life is complicated. Things are not what they seem, but I am not emotionally capable of going into deep details at this time. Rick has been doing things behind my back. I love him but I am broken by the things he has done. And I must tell you that I am three months pregnant. I would like for us to keep in touch and rebuild our friendship, but I can't even think about anything else right now. I need time for me, the baby, and to truly sort things out."

"Karmen, you deserve the best of everything life has to offer. You don't deserve to be hurt like this. I am so sorry this has happened to you. What are your plans concerning the baby?"

"I am going to have the baby. Briana is supporting me through this process. I am sure my family and other friends will also. Honestly, I haven't thought too far ahead. Financially I am secure, so the baby will be fine. I haven't thought about what the next steps are. Rick and I haven't had a transparent conversation about this because I am not entertaining what he has to say right now."

They walked a bit more and then Justin said something that grappled her heartstrings, "Karmen, may I pray for you before I take you back to your car? I only want the best for you. I know our lives drifted apart, I just want us to build our friendship again. One of the things that always gets me through tough times is my faith in God and prayer. His Word never changes, and I know that He will guide you through this difficult season. So, may I? Pray for you?"

Blown away by his request, she whispered, "*yes.*"

Abba Father, You alone are worthy to be praised. I honor and adore You. Nothing is greater than You and You are not surprised by anything we go through. You knew that this day would come, and You have prepared us for it.

Father, I ask that You strengthen Your daughter according to Your Word and help her to lean not to her own understanding but trust You wholeheartedly to perform Your Word in her life. Help her faith not to fail.

She doesn't understand the circumstance but help her to understand Your will for this situation and know that Your will is perfect. I pray that You will protect her and give her peace that surpasses all understanding. Give her wisdom and insight to make the right decisions concerning her marriage and her life moving forward.

Your Word is true, and You do not lie. You do not fail. You do not disappoint. We thank you for total healing in her life now and, Father, forgive both of us for the mistakes we have made. Thank you for loving us enough to protect us from things that are harmful to our lives. We ask these things in your Son Jesus' name. Amen."

Tears were flowing down her cheeks. It had been several months since Rick had prayed for her and she didn't think anything of it until this moment. Her soul longed for this type of covering, this type of man. Her thoughts were flooded as Justin wiped the tears rolling down her face.

"Thank you, Justin. Thank you for this refreshing evening, for being a perfect gentleman. I had no idea that you prayed this way. I don't know what tomorrow holds but I know that I feel much better than I did."

"Karmen, after going through so many obstacles in my

life, I felt it was time to surrender my life to Christ for real. I believed in Him, I said that I loved Him, yet I wasn't fully living it. Now I do. I have been preaching for several years now and pretty soon will have my own church to pastor. For many years I ran from my purpose. However, several bumps in the road led me right back to Him. My life is nothing without Him."

"Wow! That's amazing Justin. Thank you for sharing with me tonight and for helping me to take my mind off things. We will keep in touch."

Justin gave Karmen his number and took hers. Not knowing when they might see each other again, Justin hugged her tightly and lightly kissed her on the forehead.

The sun started to rise. Karmen couldn't believe they talked all night into the early morning. Justin drove her to the car and hugged her once more. "I will always love you, Karmen, even if it means from a distance. This is a new beginning, even if it is just friendship. Please text me and let me know when you have made it back to the beach house and then when you get home to Atlanta, *please?*"

"I will. Thank you again, good night—well, good morning," she chuckled.

"Good morning, Karmen. Get some rest. Tell Briana I said it was great to see her again."

"I will."

CHAPTER 5

*K*armen checked her phone. Rick had called several times while she was out. She left the phone purposefully so that she could enjoy the evening without feeling obligated to answer. She resolved in her mind and heart that she would call him later today and hear what more he had to say. It was time to listen and begin the healing process. She still wanted a divorce. Nonetheless, she wanted to give him a chance to explain himself.

Briana was up cooking breakfast. Her usual thing for retreats. "How was your evening, chica?" Laughing she said, "you stayed out all night, it must have been pretty great."

"Bri, girl you won't believe it. We talked and walked all night. And then at the end of the night, *he prayed for me*. Can you believe that? Justin praying for me?"

"Wow! No, I can't believe it, chica. I guess things have changed over the years. I mean, he's always been a *'church boy,'* just not like that."

"I know. It was incredible. I felt so peaceful and calm with him — at ease and safe. Truly amazing evening. We exchanged phone numbers and will keep in touch. I told him a little about Rick, no details, but that there were some things I had discovered. He told me that he will always love me. We agreed to just rebuild our friendship, although we can't pick up where we left off. We could mend our friendship."

"That's great, Karmen. Maybe that is what you need right now. Just a good male friend. Nothing crazy until you figure out what you are going to do about your marriage."

"Oh, I am leaving him! However, I want him to explain himself first. I want to understand why he threw our lives away."

"Good. The two of you need to talk and clear the air. Rick does have some explaining to do," she said in her Ricky Ricardo voice.

They both laughed so hard. Karmen was glad to have good friends and she was just as glad that she ran into Justin.

Whew, what a blessing to see that man again, she thought. "Let's eat, girl, and then I need a nap before I call Rick. I need all my strength not to curse him out."

They laughed again.

"But seriously Briana, I know I will have to forgive him. I just don't want the marriage anymore. Not after he's cheated on me with more than one woman. Thank you again for being here. I truly appreciate it and I am sure your niece or nephew is loving all this good food."

Briana laughed. "You are welcome, chica. You will get through this. God has a plan. And we will help you get through it. Love you, girl."

CHAPTER 6

*A*fter her nap, Karmen dreadfully decided she'd call Rick. Several hours had passed. Of course, he had called again. She checked the messages before dialing— *Karmen, baby, please let me explain. The woman that is pregnant. Baby, it's not what you think. Please let me explain. You wouldn't let me explain.*

She reminisced on the wedding, the basket of promises. Her heart and mind began to recall each promise. At this moment, she wondered if they ever meant anything to Rick. Until now, those promises represented the theme of love resonating throughout their relationship and marriage.

Blah, blah, blah, she thought. Her silent thoughts screamed, *I don't care! Even if there is more to that story, I just don't care. The fact remains he's been cheating. I don't want the marriage anymore.*

Karmen sat still for a moment and then out of thin air she heard these words, *Daughter it is your choice. Your husband is and will always be your brother in Christ first and foremost. He is my son and it is your choice. He is who he is and who I created him to be. He just won't change until he is ready. He's been this way. You just didn't hearken unto my words.*

Karmen cried desperately, *Father, I am sorry. Please forgive me. Please forgive me for not listening to you. I thought I could change him. I thought I could make him love me and only me.*

She dialed Rick's number. Still crying, she waited for him to answer.

"Baby, hello."

Karmen paused a moment before responding. Tears were still flowing down her face. "Hello, Rick. I am listening to you now."

"Karmen please forgive me for what I've done. I am so sorry. I can't make up for any of this but please let me explain the woman in Texas. She trapped me. She came into town with one of her friends. We went out and I was drinking. I am sorry. I didn't know what happened. She basically took advantage of me and now she's claiming I am the father of her baby. She posted pictures and told her family I asked her to marry me. I promise you I didn't ask her to marry me. It was a one-night stand."

"Does that make it any better Rick? You still violated

my trust, our marriage, our home, our family. That doesn't make it better. It does explain that situation. BUT it is not better. And what about the other woman or women? How do you explain them?"

"I can't Karmen. I have to take full ownership for that. I messed up and I don't blame you for being angry. You have every right to be. I thought I could handle everything and just let it go whenever I wanted. They were flings. I don't want those women."

"Rick, I don't believe you. You have truly hurt me and even though I love you, I am done with this marriage. I know God hates divorce, but He also hates lying and cheating. He hates abuse and this is abusive. I will allow you in the baby's life and I want you to be there as his or her father, but you and I are done."

"Karmen, please. Baby, please don't walk out on us. Please give me another chance."

"No, Rick, we should have never gotten married. You have been this way for years, even before we married. I knew there were other women. I just looked the other way and ignored what I knew deep inside my heart. I will have my attorney contact yours so that we can move forward and put all of this behind us."

"How can you just walk out on me like this, Karmen? What about our family?"

"Walk out on you? Rick, are you serious? You walked out on us a long time ago, the first time you cheated on me.

Don't throw this guilt trip on me. You knew what you were doing, and you did it anyway. We are done. I've heard you. I forgive you but not to save this marriage. I forgive you so that I can heal and move on with my life and for the sake of our baby. I am sure there is a lesson in this somewhere, I am just not sure what it is right now. Goodbye, Rick."

She didn't give him time to say anything else, she disconnected the call.

Though crying and broken, she felt relieved. It wasn't over, but she knew she could move forward. She gave her best. Karmen was perfectly imperfect, yet she refused to accept the responsibility of Rick being unfaithful. It was time to put the broken pieces back together, and she was going to do just that with God's help.

CHAPTER 7

A year had passed since Karmen and Rick divorced. She had given birth to a handsome baby boy and named him Micah Jeremiah. Rick wanted her to name him Rick Jr., however, she refused. Many things had changed, including selling one of her properties in Atlanta to ensure she could financially take care of herself and Micah. She didn't want to go back to work immediately after maternity leave.

Her worries and anxiety ceased. Over the past year and several months, she and Justin had built a strong friendship based on trust and unconditional respect, and love as Christ loved them. Karmen never imagined experiencing this magnitude of selfless, pure, and unconditional regard from a man. He was simply there to support her through the process. No strings, no pressure. He honored her independence and desire for time to heal and, in many ways, he needed time also. The two of them focused on building friendship and re-establishing the broken pieces of their lives. She learned to love herself again. She poured love into herself and into Micah, she began to worship and praise as she once did, faithfully serving in the ministry again. She focused on the things that mattered most now and that was building the Kingdom and building a new life with her baby boy.

"I know the plans I have for you, plans to prosper you
and not to harm you, plans to give you a hope
and a future, an expected end."
-Jeremiah 29:11

She continued to return to Savannah for vacations and special occasions. With each trip, she filled her basket with new promises, to herself, to Micah, and to God. She reflected on each promise, repurposing the basket for new beginnings, remembering that God's promises and purposes were greater than hers, and just like Briana said, "God has a plan."

TWO HEARTS UNITED

TAMALA COLEMAN

SCENE ONE

*A*nxiously sitting in the doctor's office, Delores and her husband Jason hold hands while other patients' names are called to be seen. Delores places her hand on Jason's hand as they wait to be called to see the doctor. It's been a long time since Jason and Delores had any good news in relation to having a baby. After all, they are both young, in love, and ready to start a family. Unfortunately, they have not been able to conceive successfully. So far, there have been three miscarriages. It was now in God's hands, and they trusted Him to make this the final turn-around.

While they wait, Delores is a little antsy and takes a walk outside of the doctor's office for some fresh air. She kisses Jason on the forehead and walks outside of the office doors into the hallway. She walks back and forth for a while and finally sits down on a sofa next to a grey-haired woman. "Hi, I'm Ms. Saddie," with a pleasant smile, she looks at Delores.

"Hi, I'm Delores." Ms. Saddie looks at Delores as if she could read her mind. Delores can feel this lady staring her down and becomes a little uncomfortable.

"Are you okay, my dear?" Ms. Saddie asks, "I'm not a mind reader or anything, but you are wearing your worries all over your face, my dear."

Delores looks at her and laughs, "wow, I did not realize that. Thank you for pointing that out to me. I'm just a little nervous about my pregnancy results, that's all. My husband and I have been waiting for quite some time now, and I guess I'm just a bit impatient right now."

"It's quite alright, deary, I understand, my daughter did the same thing before she had her first child."

"Is your daughter okay?" Delores asks.

"Oh, yes!" Ms. Saddie replies. "Trina is fine, that's my daughter. She just keeps having babies, but that's quite alright, I love my grandbabies."

"The doctor is ready for us now, baby," says Jason.

"Okay, sweetie. I'll be right in. It was very nice meeting you, Ms. Saddie," Dolores replies.

"You too, deary. Take care of yourself now."

Delores and Jason enter the doctor's exam room. It has been over two years since the last miscarriage. Dr. Jeffreys has been Delores' gynecologist for years since she was eighteen years old. So, the couple definitely had a trusting relationship with him.

"So, how is the beautiful couple doing this morning?"

"We are doing well," replies Delores. "So, give it to us, Dr. Jeffreys. Are we pregnant or not?"

"Well, things look very promising. I have reviewed your blood levels and your chart, Delores. It seems you have been sticking to the regiment that I gave you by eating right and resting since the last visit. You are indeed pregnant, Delores, and you are at six weeks right now."

Jason reaches over and hugs Delores as she lies on the exam table. They are overjoyed to hear the news, yet Delores still has a little doubt. Dr. Jeffreys tries to reassure the couple that with much rest and maintaining her stress levels, this time will be different, "you have to take it easy, Delores."

"I will, Dr. Jeffreys. I'm not risking anything this time."

"Unfortunately, you may need to consider not working for the duration of this pregnancy."

"I'm not sure I can leave my job right now."

"Baby, we will manage," from Jason.

"I will let you two talk about it, but this is very detrimental to your health and the baby's health. I will see you back here in a few weeks."

Jason and Delores leave the exam room and make the next appointment. As they enter the waiting room again, Ms. Saddie and her daughter Trina are walking out. Ms. Saddie sees Delores and introduces her to Trina, "my mother didn't talk your ears off, did she?"

Delores giggles, "Oh no. She was fine. I really enjoyed talking with your mom. We had a great conversation, and she's a beautiful lady."

"I'm glad," replies Trina.

Delores and Jason say their goodbyes and exit the office.

SCENE TWO

The next day, Delores plans her day with a little shopping. Even with the news of her pregnancy, the miscarriages are still fresh in her mind. Yet, Delores was not quite ready to give up. She drives up to a nearby baby clothing store and sits in her car, deciding whether to go in or not. She finally exits her car and walks into the store. As Delores walks in, the store clerk walks up and greets her with a broad smile as though she was happy to see Delores. The clerk politely asks if Delores needs any help to find anything.

Delores politely replies, "No, I am just looking."

"Well, let me know if you need anything," the clerk says and walks off.

Delores walks around the store, looking at all of the colorful, soft baby clothes, strollers, baby seats, and toys. There is a feeling of hope in her heart as she looks through all of the baby clothes and feels the soft, cozy material. Delores now has the spirit of expectancy, believing this time she will be holding a little bundle of joy finally. While walking around the store, she picks up a lovely pink onesie, places it up to her nose, and embraces the smell of the clothing. Her eyes begin to fill up with tears instantly.

The clerk sees Delores and asks if she is okay. She offers a Kleenex and takes her to a nearby seating area. At the same time, the doorbell rings as another customer walks in, and the clerk leaves her to help the lady in the store.

As Delores gathers herself together, she walks towards the door, at which time she hears someone call out her name. She turns around to see Ms. Saddie, the woman from the doctor's office. Ms. Saddie walks over cheerfully and hugs Delores tightly.

"Now, what are the chances we would meet up again here? How are you, my dear?"

Delores replies, "I'm doing well. How are you? It's Saddie, right?"

"Yes, you remembered. Are you sure you are okay? It looks like you've been crying."

"Just a little, but I'm okay now."

"So, are you leaving now?" asks Saddie. "Stay just a little bit with me. I may need some help picking out an outfit for my grandbaby, and I would love to chat with you some more."

Delores hesitates a little, but she follows Saddie through the store anyway. "So, how have you been, Delores? You really look good, but you seem distracted. Are you feeling okay?"

Delores smiles, "yes, I'm feeling well. I just had a moment while I was looking through the store, that's all."

Saddie places her hand on Delores' shoulder. "Oh, precious, you will be okay. The Lord always makes a way. Come have a seat, my poor feet are tired, and this old lady needs to sit down for a minute. So how is the hubby doing? It's Jason, right?"

"Yes, he's doing just fine. He's working today."

"You know, you two make a beautiful couple. I pray that everything works out with the new baby." This only strikes Delores at the core again as she suddenly begins to cry.

"What's the matter, baby?" Saddie looks puzzled, not sure why Delores is crying.

"I'm okay, I promise. I'm okay."

"Don't worry, sweetheart, just trust God and pray about it. And stop crying; you don't want to stress yourself. You know my daughter Trina was the same way before she finally had her first child. She would cry at the drop of a hat. I know you are worried, Delores, but don't let it bother you to the point that you miss out on the journey and the joy that comes with pregnancy. It's a beautiful thing that God has given to us women, you know?"

Delores wipes her tears, "Yes, ma'am. I'm sorry."

"No need to apologize, I have seen it all. This old woman has been around. You know, Delores, you remind me of my daughter Trina. You two would really hit it off as friends."

Delores just laughs as she stands up, grabs her handbag, and prepares to leave, "well, I better be going. It was nice seeing you again, Ms. Saddie."

"You too," replies Ms. Saddie.

As Delores walks out, Ms. Saddie shouts, "Hey, if you and your husband aren't doing anything tonight, I am having a little cookout at my house. I would love for you to come."

"Of course, I will ask Jason when I get home."

"Great, here's my address and phone number. Hope to see you both tonight."

SCENE THREE

elores arrives home, and since there are so many things running through her head with the pregnancy, she fails to see Jason's car in the driveway. He's home early. As Delores walks in, she hears a lot of noise like a drill upstairs, and she slowly walks up the stairs to the bedroom, which was once a baby room before her miscarriage some years ago. Delores has tried to avoid going into this room. She pushes the door open, and she sees Jason putting a baby bed together. Jason looks up and drops what he's doing, and walks over to Delores with his arms open wide and a goofy smile on his face.

"What is all of this?" Delores asks.

Jason replies, "I took half the day off to surprise you. We can't give up hope, baby, we just can't."

Delores takes a seat in a chair and begins to sob so hard

that Jason is confused and bewildered, "baby, I thought this would cheer you up."

"I know, Jason. It's been a long day. I think I'm just having some hormonal issues, and I just can't stop crying, I'm sorry. Thank you for doing this, Jason. It's a great surprise. It is going to take some time to readjust, that's all." Delores wipes her eyes and stands up, "I'm going take a nap for a while."

As she walks out, she remembers the invitation to Ms. Saddie's. "Oh, and we have been invited to Ms. Saddie's house for dinner tonight. You remember the lady from Dr. Jeffreys' office and her daughter? Are you okay with that?"

Jason asks how that came about.

"Well, earlier today, I was at Joy's Baby Clothing Store, and she was there too.

"That's weird how you two keep meeting. But yes, we can go if you feel up to it, baby."

"Okay, sweetie."

Later that night, Jason and Delores arrive at Maddie's house. Trina opens the door and has a look of surprise on her face. She invites them in, and they exchange hugs as she closes the door. Ms. Saddie walks up at that moment, so excited to see them. She hugs and invites them in and begins to introduce them to her other guests. "So, Delores, how are you feeling?" Ms. Saddie asks.

"I'm feeling much better, thank you," replies Delores.

"Can I get you two something to drink?"

"Yes, a glass of water would be nice, please."

"No problem, deary. You all make yourselves at home."

Meanwhile, Trina walks up and introduces her two little kids to Jason and Delores, "here are my two little angels, Patrick and Denise. They are two and five years old."

"Hello," says Delores. "They are very cute."

"They are not always like this. They are a little shy because of the company right now. But just wait, they will soon turn up the place."

They all laugh. "So, how is the pregnancy going?" Trina asks.

"It's okay right now, I guess. I'm just having episodes of crying, that's all."

"Oh yeah! I have been there and done that, but it will pass after a while. All the emotions tend to take a toll on us."

"It sure does."

In the meantime, Ms. Saddie announces that dinner is ready. Delores asks where the bathroom is, and Trina points her to the hallway.

As Delores walks down the hall, she sees a few pictures hanging on the wall. One photo especially sticks out to her, almost as if she was looking in a mirror. Trina walks up and identifies the picture on the wall as her maternal grandmother. Delores is very quiet until there is another call for dinner. Delores continues to the bathroom. She enters the dining area afterward and sits at the table next to Jason. Jason whispers and asks what took her so long. Delores never answers him.

After dinner, Ms. Saddie calls for dessert, but Delores and Jason decide to leave as it was getting late, and Delores was exhausted. As they prepare to leave, Ms. Saddie walks the couple to the door, thanking them for coming. She hands Delores her number on a piece of paper, and Delores gives her their phone number. As they continue to walk out the door, Ms. Saddie whispers to Delores, "call me."

SCENE FOUR

*J*ason and Delores say goodbye and head to the car. While driving, Jason asks Delores what happened and what did she need to talk about. Delores takes a deep breath, and with hesitation and reluctance, she mentions the picture she saw in the hallway. As she tries to utter the words, she finally said, "I think Ms. Saddie is my mother."

Jason replies, "What? Why would you think that?"

Delores, at this moment, is a little spaced out just to even speak of it. "I saw a picture on the wall as I was going to the bathroom, and the woman in the picture looked exactly like me. I mean, I thought I was looking at myself in a mirror, and Trina walks up and tells me it was her grandmother."

Jason looks at Delores, very confused as he thinks Delores is a little delirious from lack of sleep. "Jason, don't look at me like that. I am serious; I felt something so real about that photo, and I don't know what to do."

Jason says, with a concerned look on his face, "Well, maybe you should give her a call. Please calm down and try not to stress yourself over it because it's not good for you and the baby."

The next day, Delores picks up the phone to call Ms. Saddie, but she hangs up the phone. As she ponders a few seconds, she places her hand on the phone, and suddenly the phone rings. Surprisingly, on the other end of the phone is Ms. Saddie. As Delores hears her voice on the phone, her hands begin to shake uncontrollably.

Meanwhile, Ms. Saddie is on the other end, yelling, "hello? Hello?"

Delores finally answers her, but she's still overwhelmed and not sure what to say, "good morning, Ms. Saddie, its Delores."

"Hi there, deary. What a coincidence! I was just thinking about you and was going to call you to meet me for a light lunch at a café on Briar Street.

"Of course, I know where that is. I would love to. See you then."

"Okay, deary, see you at noon."

"Okay, see you soon, Ms. Saddie."

As Delores hangs up the phone, she becomes a bit anxious, so she begins to pray for strength, and also in hopes that she's not crazy to think that Ms. Saddie may indeed be her biological mother. Although Delores has never admitted it, it has always been in the back of mind who her real mother was and why she gave her up for adoption. There are so many questions running through her mind right now.

Delores arrives at the restaurant for lunch, and as she walks in, she notices Trina and Ms. Saddie waiting. She was not aware that Trina would be having lunch as well. The turn of events is beginning to become stranger and stranger for Delores. As they sit at their table, Ms. Saddie has a funny look on her face, almost as if she has seen an angel. She reaches out and hugs Delores, and so does Trina. Delores tells Trina that she was surprised to see her, and Trina responds to Delores by acknowledging she was glad to see her as well.

The waiter walks up, takes their orders, and comes back with glasses of water. Afterward, there is a period of silence until Ms. Saddie suddenly asks Delores about her birth mother. At this very moment, Delores is caught off guard, yet in her mind, she's glad that Ms. Saddie brought up the conversation so that she can put her mind to rest.

Delores takes a sip of water, and she tries to compose herself as she answers Ms. Saddie's questions, "well, there's not much to tell you. My mother gave me up at birth, but I do not have all the details surrounding what happened and why she decided to give me up."

Saddie has a sad look on her face then asks Delores another question. "May I ask how old you are?"

"No, I don't mind. I just turned 35 years old on May 18."

Trina accidentally knocks over her glass of water to the floor, and it startles everyone for a minute. The waiter walks over to the table and cleans up the table with a cloth.

Meanwhile, Delores is at the point where she needs to be clear about what she is thinking. So she looks at Ms. Saddie and blurts out, "Are you my mother?"

Caught by surprise, with tears rolling down her face, Ms. Saddie quietly says, "Yes, I think you are my daughter."

Trina then turns to Delores and lets her know that her mother has been looking for her and that this time, she also feels very strongly that she and Delores may indeed be sisters. Delores is not very surprised but indeed wants more answers.

"Delores, I have felt a deep spiritual connection with you since I met you, but I was waiting for the right time to let you know that I had a beautiful baby girl when I was younger. I could not take care of her properly, so I gave her up for adoption, and I never saw her again. I think about her often, and everyone I see, I wonder if she is the daughter I gave up."

"So what do we do now?" asks Delores. "Ms. Saddie, let's do a DNA test so that all of our minds can be at ease."

"I think that's where we need to start first," replies Ms. Saddie.

All at once, all three ladies finally exhale, but there were so many unanswered questions to be addressed. Delores has a lot of questions, so without hesitation, she poses the question to Ms. Maddie, asking if she could at least give her the history of why she gave up her daughter. Even if she is not her daughter, she wanted to know why. Ms. Saddie takes a sip of water and stares off a little bit before answering Delores.

She begins slowly as she tries to explain her past without crying, "Well, I must tell you that I was very young and I was in love with my college sweetheart. I was only twenty-one years old, but I had to drop out of school because my father was sick, and my mom was unable to care for him alone. It was a very hard time for me, and I did not find out that I was pregnant until a month after I left school."

She pauses and then continues, "The decision to give up my precious baby girl was devastating for me, to say the least. As a young caregiver to both of my parents, I was overwhelmed with the stress of it all. I was determined to find a great home for my baby, so the adoption agency assured me that a good home would be provided. I only wanted the best for my little girl since I could not afford to take care of her. I wanted her to be given love and opportunity for the best."

As Ms. Saddie speaks, her voice trembles, and as she looks in Delores' eyes, she can see tears forming as well. Ms. Saddie grabs her hand on the table and says that if she is indeed her daughter, she is asking for her forgiveness and that all that matters is that they have found each other.

With tears in her eyes, Delores replies, "I forgive you," before reaching out to hug Ms. Saddie. Before long, there wasn't a dry eye at the table.

As they sit in silence for a few moments, Trina asks her mother, "Whatever happened to your boyfriend? Did he know about the baby?"

Ms. Saddie looks at both of them and bursts out crying uncontrollably. She tries to compose herself enough to tell them what happened.

She takes a deep breath and replies, "his name was Jeremy. I loved him so much, and we had planned to get married right out of college. Things did not work as we wanted it. After I left school, he continued his education but close to graduation, he was killed in an automobile accident. He did know about the baby, and he did not talk me out of what I had decided to do, so he did have a chance to see our baby girl before he died. I lost the love of my life and our baby."

Trina goes over to her mother and hugs her to console her.

Delores says, "I'm sorry, Ms. Saddie, and I want you to know that you have a heart of gold."

Ms. Saddie and Delores agree to meet at a local doctor's office to complete DNA testing. Everything seems to be moving quickly for Delores and Ms. Saddie, yet only God knows how things will come together. Delores spends the next few days resting, as all of this has become very overwhelming for her, and she needs to relax.

SCENE FIVE

During this time, there is no communication between Delores and Ms. Saddie, until the day a letter is delivered to them both. Delores decides not to open her letter and drives to Ms. Saddie's house so that they can share the news together.

Ms. Saddie sees her coming up the walkway when opens the door while holding an open envelope. The anxiety of finding out if Delores was definitely her daughter got the best of her, and she had already opened the letter.

As Delores gets closer, she notices the open envelope, but there was no need to wonder any longer because the look on Ms. Saddie's face was unmistakable. Ms. Saddie runs up to Delores, screaming at the top of her lungs, "You're my baby, Delores! You're my baby!"

Delores is in so much shock that she nearly passes out.

"What! What! Oh, my God!" Trina stands at the door as they walk back to the house. She takes Delores by the hand and hugs her and embraces her as her sister.

"I need a drink of water, please," Delores says.

"Sure, baby." Ms. Saddie brings her a glass of water.

"This is just too surreal right now," Delores says.

"I know, baby, but God knew about it all, and it's not up to us to try to figure it all out. We just need to embrace the fact that we have finally found each other," Ms. Saddie replies.

Delores tries to stand up, but stumbles a bit and grabs her head, "I'm not feeling so well, can you all take me to the hospital?"

"Yes, baby, come on. Trina, please call Jason and tell him to meet us at the hospital."

They finally arrive at the hospital, and a nurse meets them at the emergency to carry Delores to an evaluation room. As they wait, Ms. Saddie never leaves Delores' side. She is right beside her bed, holding her hand. A few minutes later, Jason arrives and runs to Delores' bedside.

"Baby, are you alright? I got here as fast as I could."

"I'm okay, sweetie. We are just waiting for Dr. Jeffreys."

"He's on his way," replies Ms. Saddie.

As Jason calms down, he finally notices Ms. Saddie and Trina. Jason looks a little confused and puzzled. Delores quickly sees the look on his face, and she answers his question without him saying anything, "Sweetie, I have some great news. Ms. Maddie is my birth mother. We just found out today from the DNA results. I think the news was a little overwhelming, and my blood pressure escalated."

Jason congratulates them, but he's more concerned about Delores' health and the baby at the moment. Dr. Jeffrey walks in, and while he has good news after reading Delores' chart, he is concerned, "Ms. Delores, what's going on?"

"Well, Dr. Jeffreys, I had a bit of news today, and I think it caused my pressure to go up a little bit. I just found out that Ms. Saddie is my birth mother."

"Wow, that is good news! This is a small world. How amazing!"

Dr. Jeffrey continues to check her blood pressure and other vitals. He takes off the pressure cuffs from Delores' arms and reminds her of his initial instructions, "go home and rest, Delores, remember what I told you. We want to bring a healthy baby into the world, and we want you to take care of yourself now, Delores."

"Yes, Dr. Jeffreys. I will, I promise."

SCENE SIX

Seven months pass, and Jason and Delores finally are the new parents of a little girl named Brandy. This is an amazing blessing for the couple and the family they always longed for, after so many years, was now a dream come true. They are preparing to take their little bundle home from the hospital when Ms. Saddie walks into Delores' room with balloons, flowers, and a Teddy Bear. She has tears in her eyes as she stands still for a moment and watches Delores holding their baby girl. Delores looks up and sees Ms. Saddie.

"Mom," Delores calls out. "Come on in and meet your new grandbaby."

Ms. Saddie walks closer, "She's so beautiful. Can I hold her?"

"Of course, you can."

As Ms. Maddie looks down at Brandy in her arms, she

is so overwhelmed that the tears will not stop flowing. "I now have my first-born daughter and an addition to my grandchildren. We are so blessed."

"Yes, we are," replies Delores. "How is Trina doing with her new baby boy, my nephew?" Delores asks.

"That little pee-wee is so adorable. I can't believe I have two new grandbabies to love."

The nurse comes in with a wheelchair to take Delores and the baby out to their car. Jason picks up the baby seat and Delores' duffle bag, "I'll meet you outside at the car."

Delores sits in the wheelchair, and Ms. Saddie hands baby Brandy to her. As they take the long walk down the hospital corridor, they decide to have a heart to heart conversation. After all, these ladies have been on a journey. God has blessed them to come together and not only bond but also connect as mother and daughter. Ms. Saddie alone has been on an emotional roller coaster, and Delores has endured heartache and loss in her lifetime. God has made it possible for their paths to cross.

The nurse stops at the elevators as they wait. Ms. Saddie looks at Delores and expresses her thankfulness for Delores. "I must tell you, Delores, I'm so very thankful that God allowed us to come together as a family, and I promise that I will love you, little baby Brandy, and Jason with my whole heart. As long as I am alive, I will be here for you."

Delores again is an emotional wreck. After finally giving birth and finding her mother, all of this has been a huge change, but she is also grateful. "Mom, I am so grateful and thankful as well. I thank God that you never stopped looking for me. I'm so glad that God orchestrated so much in our paths crossing. I am happy to be your daughter."

Two hearts united... a story of *hope*, *faith*, and *endurance*. When God orchestrates things, it always turns out good. Hearts are restored from being lost and found from darkness to light.

ABOUT THE
AUTHORS

SANDRA ASTACIO

PASTOR SANDRA ASTACIO is a life-long resident of Florida and proudly calls Lakeland her home. She and her husband, Antonio, just celebrated ten years of marriage and they have a blended family of all boys and two grandsons.

After earning her Christian Leader's Certificate from the globally recognized Bible Training Centre for Pastors, she became an ordained Pastor in 2016. In late 2018, Sandra published her first book, "In Pursuit of Becoming: One Woman's Journey to Herself'" which she tells of powerful life stories intertwined with biblical teaching, prophetic prayers, and inspiring poetry.

She is the Founder and President of *Daughters in Christ Ministries, Inc. —A Christian Ministry for Women* where she offers Community Volunteer Training, Ministerial Services, Career Preparation Services, Administration Services, Biblical Studies Online, and much more! The vision of the ministry is to Inspire, Encourage, and Empower Christian women of faith to live fully as a

Daughter in Christ and to walk boldly in whom Christ has created them to be.

Pastor Sandra strives consistently to help women capture this vision while allowing the Spirit of God to expand her territory as a respected Christian leader within her community and beyond.

For booking or more information:
www.DaughtersinChrist.com

TAMALA COLEMAN

LADY TAMALA J. COLEMAN is a Best Selling Author, Playwright, and Podcast Radio Host. She has written several books, including: "Spiritual Expressions" Poetry Book, "Divine Women of God" Devotional for Women, "Woman in the Mirror", Co-Author of "Unleashed Travails" From Pain to Purpose, "Donovan Shoes" Children's Book, Co-Author of 365 Women's Devotional, "Unspoken" Memoir her life story.

As the Podcast Radio Host of "Spiritually Speaking with Tamala Coleman" on iTunes, Spreaker, iHeart Radio, she won the Radio Personality of the Year for the ACHI Magazine Awards for 2019. Tamala is also the owner of TC Praise Productions, LLC in which she has produced stage plays "Lord Change My Heart" and "He Who Finds a Good Thing."

Tamala has been featured in the Writers Life Magazine and Featured Cover, Voyage ATL Magazine, several radio interviews: "Fire" The Gospel Experience Radio show with Ron Jefferson, Dr. Sharon Hargro Porter on "Write the Book Now" Talk Show and Youtube Channel Authors Interview with JeQuita Zachary Johnson.

Tamala attended Ames International Biblical Ministry School in 2011, where she earned a Diploma/Certification in Biblical Studies and holds a General Ministerial License through Ames Biblical College. Tamala enjoys spending time with her family, teaching and encouraging others with the Word of God.

For booking or more information:
www.tamalacolemanbooks.yolasite.com

SHELLY SHELTON

LADY SHELLY SHELTON is a well-known women's empowerment and corporate-focused motivational speaker, an accountability specialist, and a talent acquisition guru! Her motto, "One woman can change the world—I am never giving up—I can do this" is nothing short of what she lives everyday in her personal and professional life.

With the confidence to say, "I AM SHELLY SHELTON", she is a published Author, the CEO of Shelly Shelton & Associates LLC, Founder of Unstoppable University, Aspiring Speakers Academy, and TLC Recruiting Academy. Shelly holds a B.S. in Business from Virginia Union University and a M.S. in Human Resources Management from Central Michigan University.

Shelly currently resides in Richmond, Virginia.

For booking or more information:
www.unstoppableuniv.com

ANGEL MILLER

LADY ANGEL MILLER is an ordained minister, Christian counselor, educator, career services provider, mental health recovery professional, and life & business Coach.

Angel is a powerhouse Entrepreneur with numerous accomplishments and awards as a business woman, Amazon bestselling author and inspirational speaker, and teaches many topics, including wellness recovery, literacy, professional development, social skills, interpersonal effectiveness and women's empowerment. She owns multiple businesses and loves her career as a sexual assault advocate in Gaston County, NC.

In her spare time she enjoys spending time with her family, friends, and her dog Angel2.

For booking or more information:
facebook.com/angelBinspired

ELAINE ROUNDTREE MONTFORD

MINISTER ELAINE ROUNDTREE MONTFORD is a prolific author and poet, with a heart for God, and a passion for creative literary expression. She is the Author of *The Birth of Victorious Destiny* and *Moving Forward in Victorious Destiny: Little Girl Steps... with Big Girl Faith.*

Elaine is also a contributing author in the best-selling anthology series "Testify" — *Unmerited Favor & Divine Provision* and *Alabaster Box.*

Additionally, Minister Montford is the Founder and Managing Partner of Montford Manuscripts, where she supports authors with alpha reading and proofreading services, and a contributing partner of DHBonner Virtual Solutions in the MOMENTUM! Publishing Division.

For booking or more information:
facebook.com/elaineroundtreemontford